UTOMIA

Caitlin Scholl
& Neil Mullins

ADAPTIVE BOOKS

AN IMPRINT OF ADAPTIVE STUDIOS | CULVER CITY, CA

Visit us on the web at www.adaptivestudios.com

Library of Congress Cataloging in Publication Number: 2018933309
ISBN 978-1-945293-69-6
Ebook ISBN 978-1-945293-70-2

Printed in the United States of America.
Designed by Neuwirth & Associates.

Adaptive Books
3733 Motor Avenue,
Los Angeles, CA 90034

10 9 8 7 6 5 4 3 2 1

for our Máithaireacha

Máthair, máthair milis,
a beathíonn an uile ní;
Is a broinn uisceach
a dhéannan sin iomlán.

Máthair, máthair foinse,
Tá mé i bhfiach duit do mo chuid ama;
Fós, do dhuine ar bith
Nílim i bhfiach do m'anam.

Mother, sweet mother,
who animates all;
whose watery womb
makes us whole.

Mother, great mother,
I owe you my time;
yet to no one
I owe my soul.

TABLE OF CONTENTS

UTOMIA

Chapter 1
THE EXPERIMENT

On what had begun as a brilliantly clear day over the village of Talamh, the sun shone its last rays upon a low, square cedar schoolhouse, perched on a northern knoll.

Inside, the scent of rich wood sap filled the air. It was about to rain. Laoch yawned and leaned his long green neck over the small desk. He placed his ear to the wood. Scratches students had made over the years—initials, declarations of love ("Brewster and Belina forever"), and statements of being ("Whistler was here")—covered the desk. He wasn't paying attention to that, though. He was feigning sleep.

Ms. Whakdak, his teacher, prattled on. A knowing smile spread across her face as she expounded on her favorite topics—namely grasses and shrubbery—as part of a seminar all students in the Southern Hills were required to pass. And while "The 4 Major Types of Grasses" was a much-anticipated class for many of his schoolmates, it was perhaps the most boring topic Laoch could imagine.

"It's not only the *biological significance* that I am speaking of, but the Rigglewok Grass's entire *placement* within grassland *hierarchies!*" she exclaimed.

Ms. Whakdak ambled across the room on thick brown haunches. She was particularly rotund—even for a Toad that was getting on in years—and the sheer volume of her voice caused her body to quiver like a bowl of jelly.

Laoch could stand neither the sight nor the sound of her.

"Now stop diddling and pay attention, everyone, I have a LOT more to cover today," she continued. "It's the lesson you've all be waiting for!" Deep creases grouped like crinkled leaves around her eyes as she squinted at the students. It was apparent that she could barely see, for Sty had hidden her glasses earlier that morning.

"And lest anyone forgets . . . WHAT are we here for, Class?"

"*Learning*, Ms. Whakdak," the pupils replied in unison.

They had heard that line before.

Satisfied for the moment, and with a decided *hmmmph*, the teacher began furiously scribbling lists and diagrams on the board.

But Laoch's mind wandered, waiting for Nudge to show up. He glanced out the window. A gentle rain had begun to fall over the stand of trees and benches not far from the schoolhouse. It was a meeting place where he and his friends congregated as often as possible—before school, after school, during lunch, sometimes even during class. No sign of Nudge. The sound of thunder resounded through the walls.

He hoped the rain wouldn't spoil the plan.

"Mmm-mm-mm-mm-mm," Ms. Whakdak hummed cheerfully, completing the final flourish on her stylized rendering of a ribbon holding together a bundle of wheat. An example of edible grass species, per the lesson at hand.

Laoch found the drawing to be totally unnecessary. Why did they need it? Everyone in the room knew what wheat looked like. They lived and breathed wheat in the Southern Hills. He wouldn't care if he never saw another grain of wheat in his entire life. Still, his teacher nodded, quite pleased with herself, and continued with her notes. The rest of the students copied them down like crazy, trying to keep up with her, drawings and all.

Keeping one eye on the window, Laoch began to scribble in his notebook. Nudge sure was taking his sweet time before giving the signal.

Farming rots your brain, he wrote in tiny looping letters. For a moment he admired the sentence, noting that his handwriting wasn't half bad. In slightly bigger letters he penned another few sentences while Ms. Whakdak droned on about seed dispersal.

An Essay on the History of Farming, he wrote.

And then:

Farming is the chosen profession of Beings who have failed at everything else in life. Whereas teaching farming is the profession of those who have also failed at farming. . . .

"You get to see something big, and useful, and beautiful grow from something very tiny. Something that bears no resemblance to the thing it becomes," his father explained only a week earlier. He extended his hand toward his son, seeds scattered across its wide, rough palm.

"I don't have any idea what you're talking about," Laoch shot back, digging his trowel into the earth. "It's just a load of shoveling and other monotonous tasks. All so we can eat food that other folks just get at the market without having to do so much work." His voice rose higher and higher until it cracked, for he was fourteen and still very much between a Childling and a grown Being.

"We provide that food to the whole community," his father replied patiently. This was a conversation they'd had before, and he was beyond being insulted by his son's distaste for the family business.

"Lizardkind are meant to be warriors—"

"Not all of them," his father said, cutting him off.

"What about Iguanas? They're part of the very best army. They *are* warriors!" Laoch proclaimed, puffing out his chest until his scales bristled softly against one another. The line of spikes atop his head, running from brow to neck, poked out a bit farther. "They basically run the entire *city*."

His father sighed, and one eye wandered off down a line of crops. He was part Chameleon, this was no question. While a majority of the Lizard families in the Southern Hills were hybrids and could only guess at the genetics of their ancestors, Chameleon blood was easy to spot. The ability to change color depending on one's surroundings or mood. Strong hands that could grip any branch or tool like a vise. And perhaps most tellingly, Laoch's father possessed the uncanny ability to swivel one eye toward the task at hand—weeding a long row of carrot-like vegetables called crupes—and one at his disgruntled teenage son.

Laoch hated this about his father.

"We don't live in that city," his father said quietly, though this was of course obvious. And while Laoch had certainly been in a challenging mood, he was not ready to open the door to a discussion about the city in question. This had happened numerous times before, and the conversations never ended well, nor quickly.

"And *furthermore*," Ms. Whakdak continued, her bulbous rear bouncing up and down as she spoke, "the sheer *magnitude* of grasses and *information* on grasses is so expansive that you could continue learning new things *about* grasses for the rest of your lives!"

Laoch tuned out Ms. Whakdak's voice as she jabbered on and on and on. He had been in school for nearly ten years, and according to his family he had ten left before he would become a Master Grower. Ms. Whakdak was, apparently, an expert at training Master Growers. Yet no one but Laoch and his friends seemed to care about the fact that she had never farmed a day in her life.

And more important: becoming a Master Grower was *not* what Laoch had in mind.

Nudge, for instance, was quitting school soon to train full time for the Water Games, which he'd join the following year when he was sixteen. Even Sty was allowed to decide whether to continue his studies or not. He actually *wanted* to become a Grower, but at least it was his own choice. Whereas Laoch had none.

His twin brother, Leeland, was in the same boat, however. He'd been taken out of school last year and sent to apprentice with a local Cobbler. Again, his parents' decision. They simply informed him one day that he was destined to make shoes, and off he went. There was no explanation as to why Leeland would be a Cobbler, nor Laoch a Master Grower.

Many times Laoch wished passionately to be any kind of Being but a Lizard. He would have given his arm (or at least a finger or claw) to have been born a Meerkat, who were not only allowed but encouraged by their families to travel and seek adventure in their youth. There were just so *many* Meerkats in each family, it didn't really seem to matter who stayed and who went. Plus, they were absolutely fanatical about sports. If a son or daughter had the chance to compete in the Water Games, well, it would be a huge boon to the whole family. Nay, the whole town.

Even Toads, for all their haughty cleverness, seemed to allow their children to find their own paths. Bat youths were almost completely independent too, save the short time they spent clinging to their mothers' bodies after birth. And while Sty had mentioned more than once that it's not all it's cracked up to be, Laoch couldn't help but envy him. For his freedom, but also (and especially) for his ability to fly.

These factors combined fed Laoch's commonly held sentiment that he just didn't care much for school at all. There were other things on his mind.

Suddenly, it happened. Nudge appeared on the bench outside the window. The scrappy Meerkat—looking like a puffy ball of fur in such humidity—was jumping up and down for dear life. He flapped his arms back and forth like a madman, a wild grin spreading across his face. The rain, stronger now, flew every which way off his shiny coat. For a moment Laoch did nothing, transfixed by the funny sight, until Nudge began to stamp his feet and howl. (Luckily, no one could hear him due to the rain, the sturdiness of the schoolhouse's thick wooden walls, and Ms. Whakdak's continued stream of encyclopedic jargon about the various species of native grasses.)

Laoch nodded and coolly ran his hand over the small spikes atop his head while Nudge—who somehow registered the signal through the blinding rain—vanished from the bench as quickly as he'd appeared. Meanwhile, Laoch placed his head back on his desk, inhaled deeply, then let out the loudest, longest snoring sound he could muster. This was the signal for Sty, who was in the back of the room.

Ms. Whakdak received the signal too.

"Who was that?!" she demanded, swiveling to face the class. One long jumping leg twitched as if to indicate her desire to pounce. Laoch didn't doubt that she was a formidable Hopper.

She aimed her glossy eyes in his direction and demanded that the offender reveal itself. Sty crouched low, and with one talented swoop flew silently out the back door, not more than a foot above the ground.

Another roll of thunder sounded dully through the walls.

Laoch jerked his head, pretending to be abruptly roused.

"Oh Ms. Whakdak!" he shouted. The rest of the students—a mix of hybrid Lizards like Laoch, some Meerkats, two Toads, and only one other Bat (Sty having slipped out unnoticed)—had already pivoted toward the back of the room, anticipating something entertaining.

"Who is that? Laoch? Were you *sleeping*? Is that Laoch or isn't it?"

Ms. Whakdak shifted her weight onto one folded leg. The full length of her hind jumper jerked out, extending almost the entire width of the classroom. It was an immodest pose. One of the Meerkats near the front of the classroom snickered.

"Hush!" she called to the class. "If you know what's good for you!" Rocking forward onto her small fronties—humorously feeble compared to her massive hind haunches—Ms. Whakdak craned her giant head down the aisle between desks.

As her squat body elongated, she opened her gaping mouth in his direction, emitting a foul-smelling odor. Toad breath was nothing to be reckoned with.

"Oh Ms. *Whakdak*," Laoch sputtered again, this time coughing. More laughs from the class.

"What do you *mean*, 'Oh Ms. Whakdak' . . . ? Have I startled you, Prince Laoch?" she scoffed sarcastically. "I believe I heard you *snoring,* which is unfortunate not only because it is, as we all know, extremely *rude* to sleep in class, but because you have missed a lot of *very important information about grasses!*"

She huffed in his face. Her semi-blind eyes twinkled, as she was well aware of the power of her breath.

"You can't find your *glasses*?!" he offered meekly, choking on the smell.

Her eyes bulged.

"No, Laoch, I *said* you're missing the lesson on *grasses!*"

"No wonder, I *thought* you were squinting! Did you misplace them? No, you must have sat on them. Or perhaps someone *stole* them—"

"*Laoch,* now don't—"

"I wonder, I wonder," he speculated, "*who* might have taken them? Was it you, Tillby?"

The other Bat sank into her chair. She was used to being wrongly accused, of course. Thus was the lot of Batkind. And though everyone was accustomed to using Tillby (and even Sty) as a scapegoat within the classroom, Laoch regretted his accusation—even though it was in jest—as soon as she ducked her little head, for she looked very meek and innocent indeed.

But there was no turning back now and no time to worry about hurt feelings.

"This is all very amusing, Laoch, but your silly antics for today are over. Why don't you go up to the front of the classroom—*since you seem to be enjoying the spotlight*—and you can instruct us on the Eight Most Resilient Qualities of Shrub Shrod."

As the young Lizard slowly made his way to the blackboard, a few of the students giggled in anticipation. He figured that about five to seven minutes had passed since Sty flew out the back door, which was the amount of time it had taken him and Nudge to complete a trial set up the night before. But that was in clear weather.

"Wouldn't you rather just give me detention?" Laoch asked, buying a little more time. Not only was the rain coming down like Anam Returned (a common expression in those parts), but the wind had kicked up something fierce. The windows rattled in their frames. *This certainly sets the mood*, he thought, hoping their plan would work. If it didn't, it would be almost a whole month of wasted time and effort. "Or, why don't I just stay after class while *you* take a nap, Ms. Whakdak . . . then we'll be even!"

"I don't need to spend any more time with you than I have already," she retorted. Despite appearances, Ms. Whakdak was no slouch. Her wit was dry and quick—both common characteristics of Toadkind in general. "Now please, Laoch, why don't you start going over the Eight Qualities that I mentioned?"

As Laoch turned to face his classmates from the front of the room, he suddenly could not move. Ms. Whakdak tapped one of her globular toes on the ground, and a sea of faces looked eagerly in his direction. He had a reputation for fearlessness and challenging authority, and yet his heart beat wildly against his chest. This he had not anticipated.

The thing was, the experiment they were about to launch was pretty big. Bigger than all the others, at least. And with potential, or even probable, risk, for Laoch nor any of his friends knew quite what would happen once it was set into motion.

"WELL?" the teacher sounded impatient.

The other students emitted a few snickers. The clock ticked on. It was now or never. So Laoch swallowed hard, took one large breath, and winked at his classmates. This produced not more laughter but rather, rapt attention.

"So YOU want ME to write on THIS board, RIGHT now. Is that correct?" he uttered haltingly, feigning embarrassment.

"Yes, Laoch, that is correct."

Ms. Whakdak jiggled with anticipation at what he'd invent, quite certain—and rightly so—that he had no idea what Shrub Shrod was.

"You're SURE you want me to do this?"

"For goodness sake, Laoch, YES!" she exclaimed.

And so Laoch wasted no more time, reaching into his belt pouch and pulling out what appeared to be a small stub of chalk. *Here goes*, he whispered (inaudible to anyone but himself and Tillby the Bat), before scribbling frantically over Ms. Whakdak's expansive notes.

As soon as his chalk—which wasn't chalk at all—touched the board, something strange began to happen.

Ms. Whakdak's notes began to flicker and glow. The entire surface became illuminated, and for a moment the students could see the word *Grasses* glitter distinctly before it was subsumed into another careening jettison of fluorescent light that continued to spread across the board.

"Ooooh," the class crooned as Laoch continued his furious scrawls. Because the daylight had grown dim with the rain, the effect was certainly heightened and the stunned faces of the students and their teacher shone in the blackboard's glow.

This was the best prank he had pulled off yet.

And it was just beginning.

Ms. Whakdak, realizing she'd been had, screamed Laoch's name just as the windows began to rattle a bit harder. The small woodstove in the corner, made of heavy iron, jerked to the right, the long metal chimney bending easily like a snake. One of the students jumped back in fear.

"Here we go! Get ready for blastoff!" Laoch yelled, waiting for the roof to levitate off the schoolhouse walls. A few students squealed with excitement, and a few others ran out of the building in a great hurry.

But as the windows rattled more and more and the stove-pipe wagged like a noodle, Laoch realized that the experiment was not going as planned.

He stopped scribbling only to watch the glowing light streaks on the board continue to pulse of their own accord and spread across the wall, running rampant as vines. They split and grew in every direction. The pattern resembled the lines of a leaf, or the veins underneath a Being's skin or scales.

"Look!" someone screamed. Laoch turned his gaze along the back wall. Billowing purple smoke had begun to rise from the windows. Afraid that the roof was catching fire from the outside, he called for Nudge and Sty. Futile. The rain and wind, the rattling windows, the shaking stove, not to mention the uproar of the students made it impossible to hear anything. The classroom was in complete chaos. Many students had run out and a few huddled in the center of the room, watching the spectacle either with awe or wide-mouthed fear. Ms. Whakdak was nowhere to be seen.

The windows, one by one, began to melt. Purple flames engulfed the glass. Curiously, the wooden frames didn't catch, but the glass slowly dripped down on itself like a candle, puddling in iridescent pools on the floor.

"Mind the glass gloop!" Ms. Whakdak yelled, suddenly re-entering the building to fetch the stragglers. "Everyone out NOW!" With that, the rest of the students ran out the back door, their teacher feverishly on their tails.

Laoch alone remained inside, mesmerized by the unexpected effects of his grandest experiment yet. Careful to avoid the glass, he fixed his eyes on the stove, which continued to behave curiously. Inside, a purple fire raged. It roared and grew, the beautiful purple flames creeping out around the edges of the door. Laoch could only imagine the purple smoke that must be pouring from the schoolhouse chimney outside.

And yet, while the flames roared and the light beams on the blackboard had all but engulfed the rest of the schoolhouse, the young Lizard felt no heat.

"Laoch!" a voice yelled.

Sty swooped in through the smoke clouds rapidly filling the room and landed next to his friend. Sirens from the local fire protectorate had begun to reverberate over the hills.

"This is amazing!" Laoch yelled back. "Do you think it's gonna rise?"

"No!" Sty shouted. "It's not working. We gotta get out of here!"

And then it became apparent.

The experiment was an utter disaster.

Chapter 2

CONVERSATIONS IN THE DARK

Night fell, and behind the four youngsters loomed a large shape in the darkness, partially lit by flickering light from their small campfire.

A towering tree house, three years in the making.

Comprised of fifteen ascending levels, triangular, and built concentrically around a very tall tree, the structure almost reached the top of the woodland canopy. Its most recent addition, a slide snaking around the entire tree house from top to bottom, raged with a flume of rainwater. Laoch and the others had been waiting for it to fill all summer, given the current drought afflicting the Southern Hills. Under normal circumstances such a sight would have filled them with excitement, and they'd be scampering around their impressive fort, riding their new waterslide with wild calls and laughter. . . .

But not now.

Breathless after fleeing the schoolhouse disaster, they hadn't said much upon reaching their secret spot. These woods—rather rare in the Southern Hills—were the boys' haven.

Nudge sat in the rain, his fur musty with wood smoke. Laoch and Sty huddled nearby, along with Leeland, Laoch's twin brother, who had joined the others once word of the catastrophe had spread throughout Talamh. (Which didn't take very long.) Leeland had been left out of the plan altogether. This was common now that he spent his days apprenticing at the Cobbler Shop while the others were in school.

"I don't understand what went wrong," Laoch moaned, and threw another branch onto the sputtering coals. The campfire was protected by a small tarp strung between adjacent saplings, but still it hissed as errant drops were flung into the struggling flames.

"It must have been the rain," Sty replied. He glanced up at a drip that was landing on his head. Warm-blooded, mammalian, the Bat shivered and leaned over the fire. "We did it the same way we practiced . . . it's just that everything was wet this time."

"No, I think it was the crystals," Laoch muttered, more to himself than to anyone else. He'd grown some completely by accident a few months back while working in his tree house laboratory, although he still didn't understand them very well.

"What crystals?" Leeland asked, but no one answered him.

Nudge, impervious to the rain because of his glossy coat, paced outside the tarp to keep watch. Not that he could see much.

The others clustered tightly beneath the small square of semidry space the tarp offered. Though Laoch and Leeland were both cold-blooded, the effects of low temperatures were not desirable. Their hearts slowed, their minds became groggy. In ancient times, perhaps before the Great Change, lizards might have simply hibernated in the cold and let their minds grow dim in a sort of dreamless sleep. But now the boys struggled to stay warm. They huddled on either side of Sty, who was also damp and quivering.

"But what was *supposed* to happen?" Leeland persisted, still confused.

"The roof was supposed to levitate. Just a little — just to scare everyone," Laoch replied. He stared into the fire, his small mohawk illuminated. "It was my best idea yet."

A few months earlier, Laoch had been alone inside his laboratory, working intensely. Outside, Nudge balanced on one toe on the top rung of a ladder. He hammered away at some new support beams underneath what would become the highest portion of the waterslide (the very last part to go up).

"Stop showing off!" Sty chided happily, winging up with more nails. Nudge, in reaction, hopped to his other toe, then exploded into the air and hammered the rest of a nail into a board before tucking into a tight ball, spinning three times in a circle, and landing on his hind haunches with both arms extended. A huge toothy grin spread across his whiskered face, and he took a bow.

"And that, ladies and gentlemen of the court, is how you do it."

"Oh shush up and come get these shingles. They're about dry, I think," Leeland called, bemused. Of the four boys he was the artist, and had painstakingly covered their fort with painted flakes of bark so that from every angle it blended into the surrounding woods.

Laoch could hear them hauling things up by way of the waterslide. His hands moved quickly, nimbly filling beakers with various substances. Pour. Mix. Stir. Vapors rose and clung together in nebulous misty masses.

He whispered to himself as he worked.

"Silver allum, magnetized to canvas stiffened with copper wires and moth dust—"

"These shingles just blend right in with all the others," Nudge muttered, nailing another to the tight outer shell. Over time they had begun to take on the quality of Lizard scales.

"Wolf's piss and milk pods, tempered along the veins of a young Smelderling—"

"That's the *point*, Nudge!"

"Apply the crushed residue of Bat hair and sulfur substrate—"

"Yeah yeah, I know, I just thought maybe it would be nice if you painted a little bird every now and then," Nudge replied, and Sty laughed out loud. The sun was setting through the trees.

"Iron water—"

"We should get going soon. What do you think?"

"And lastly, the crystals—"

"Yeah, I'm hungry. Go get Laoch, will you?"

But then it happened. The bottle in which Laoch had created this concoction began . . . somehow . . . to float.

"Guys!" he cried. "Guys, you gotta see this! Come quick!"

"But how were you going to get the *roof* to rise?" Leeland exclaimed. To him this was a fool's mission. Besides, he preferred roofs that were *attached* to the walls.

"It has to do with the bottle I levitated. Remember? And those crystals I grew ... and *another* material I found ... this chalky stuff," Laoch explained. "When you put them together, it creates a charge, so—"

"I have *no clue* how it works," Nudge interrupted. "Purple flames? Total mistake!" Besides Laoch, the boys mostly had no idea why or how these experiments worked. "But did you *see* Whakdak's face?" he continued. "She just about cracked a leg!"

The others laughed, recalling their teacher's horror, while Nudge—who needed frequent outlets for his extra energy—pounced on Laoch, t, tackling him in mock battle. "*Oh, Laoch, STOP that!*" he squealed, imitating the inimitable Toad Whakdak.

Laoch squirmed out from under the furry flesh and knocked him sideways with his tail.

"Whakdak's probably a *much* better fighter than you, my friend," he shot back. "You'll never make it in the Water Games if this is all you've got." The Meerkat pounced again, as only Meerkatkind can, and Laoch was thrown back against one of the trees supporting the tarp.

"Knock it off!" Leeluul grumbled, a huge stream of water falling on his and Sty's heads. "This tarp is pointless if you keep bumping into it."

Sty flew off and perched just inside the tree house, though still within earshot. He didn't mind the others' shenanigans, but he didn't participate. It wasn't the way of Bats to rough-house like that.

Laoch flattened his body to the ground, playing dead for a moment. Nudge could never help himself even though Laoch had used this trick on him countless times before. He jumped on the Lizard's belly, and before he knew it was flipped over and smooshed underneath a pile of damp leaves.

"Fine! You win!" he yelled, wildly thrashing his arms and legs.

Laoch backed off and plopped down next to his brother, heart pumping and body warmed from the skirmish.

"Don't you think we should go home?" Leeland asked.

Laoch laughed acerbically. "NO!" he yelled. "Well, *you* can go, I suppose, but I certainly can't. Mother and Father are going to be busting out of their scales at me for this one."

"The whole town is probably upset!" Nudge added, brushing leaves off his coat and straightening the red bandanna around his neck (though it was rare for it not to be askew). He didn't care too much about the trouble they were in since he'd be off to the Cascade Sea soon enough. "What do you think, Siy?"

"I think they're probably a bit upset," Siy called from his dark perch. He had the most common sense of them all. "But mostly, they're probably relieved that the rain finally came."

Laoch realized that Siy was right. Despite the mayhem they'd caused, the Beings of Talamh were probably ecstatic that

23

the drought had finally ended and their crops would be saved. Sty too was happy about this. For unlike Laoch, he was already an Apprentice Grower and cared very much for the fine tract of fruit trees he helped tend on the western ridge just outside of town.

Still, this thought rested uneasily in Laoch's mind. For he'd hoped the drought would continue, and that he'd prove his father wrong once and for all: that farming was not a viable career path for him, or anyone else for that matter.

"Hey Laoch, why don't you grow another crystal and use it to stop this rain?" Leeland asked, feeling very damp and dismal indeed.

But Laoch just scowled at him and stalked off. He entered the tree house by feel (for it was pitch dark away from the fire), and passed Sty without even knowing it. Grasping along the walls, he ascended until he reached his laboratory, where he lit a small candle. Instantly the room was illuminated. Remnants of his recent experiments were scattered in jars upon odd tables and shelves, salvaged long ago from his father's shed and the rubbish heaps just outside of town. Still, Laoch's assemblage of lab equipment paled in comparison to the ever-growing collection of specimens they held. Stones. Leaves. Soil. Roots. Dew from the center of a just-bloomed flower.

When he was very young, he would combine substances like these purely by accident. Throwing bath salts into a bucket of manure, then watering it. The spores that grew kept the cows walking batty for days. Then there was the time he placed a stone into his father's evening tonic and it began to boil. His parents had admonished him, baffled.

But nowadays, Laoch had learned to predict these reactions. To direct the outcomes. And each time this happened, an exhilarated *whoosh* would course through his body.

But now he merely looked upon the great mess he had created. *All my work these past few months . . . wasted*, he thought angrily. The schoolhouse experiment was an utter failure, not the shining example of genius he'd hoped it would be. For inventing something truly profound was no small feat. And that was all that Laoch would accept.

He picked up the nearest jar and threw it against the wall.

The others heard the crash, and silence took over the camp. The remaining boys left the fireside, nimbly finding their way up the tree house to the middle floor, where, away from the fire, all three felt the chill of night. Each dove into his own bunk and lay there for a minute or two, listening to the rain. Soon Laoch joined them (although no one mentioned the smashing sound). They were enveloped by darkness. Eventually they lay still and listened to the water rushing down the slide, splattering on the ground below. The sound of this lulled the three boys to sleep, while Sty, awake as always in the night hours, kept vigil.

Chapter 3

THE FIRE THAT WOULDN'T GO OUT

"It was your son!" Ms. Whakdak yelled, pointing her long, warty finger. "He's done it again! What do you have to say about *that*?!"

Laoch's father (who'd arrived on the scene as soon as he heard there was trouble at the schoolhouse, knowing full well who was probably behind it) swiveled an eye at the Toad.

"I'd say he managed to get your attention."

A ripple of laughter cascaded among the onlookers and Fire Marshals both, everyone grateful for a little levity in what was becoming an increasingly tense situation. While one of the Marshals—a fatherly Meerkat—tried to calm the flustered teacher, Laoch's father ogled the smoking building with one eye and scanned the crowd with the other. He didn't expect to see his son there, however, and had a feeling that Laoch would not be home that night. Indeed, he knew of the boys' tree house (which was not much of a secret, though he allowed them to believe it was).

As Ms. Whakdak's impassioned huffing and puffing got huffier and puffier by the moment, the Fire Marshal, fearing her eventual collapse, rested his paw kindly on her wide back. She hopped away brusquely.

Laoch's father sighed. He'd been through scenes like this with her before.

"Oh you *would* say that!" she yelled. "You have *no* idea what he disrupted today, nor have you any control over him."

"Nor have you, over your students."

More laughter.

"*Oh oh, OH!*" she squealed. "I see, like Father like Son . . . you think this is all one big joke."

"Now, Ms. Whakdak—" one of the Marshals, and a friend of Laoch's father, interjected.

"No no, it's fine," his father replied. "Ms. Whakdak, I assure you I do not think this is funny in the slightest. Laoch will have a long row to hoe tomorrow morning, and probably the morning after that as well. He will not go unpunished."

"That's the problem with the lot of you!" she hollered, her mottled visage turning a deeper shade of brown. "Using the

27

sacred art of farming as *punishment!*" With that, Ms. Whakdak turned back to the fatherly Fire Marshal, her eyes evermore squinty (for her spectacles were still stashed wherever Sty had hidden them earlier), and made a sound like *HMMMPH*.

"But what are you going to do about ... about ... about the *fire*?" a voice stuttered from somewhere within the crowd.

The Fire Marshals looked at one another but said nothing. Then the Head Marshal stepped forward.

"Everyone should know that we have everything under control!" he boomed.

The crowd mumbled.

"Yeah right—" someone hissed.

"Then put it out!" called another.

"It is thoroughly contained!" the Head Marshal continued, puffing his chest out a little farther. He in no uncertain terms knew either of these proclamations to be true, but he had a very convincing manner of speaking. And so he continued explaining exactly how everything was perfectly fine, and eventually the crowd quieted, sufficiently calmed.

The other Marshals who had been on the scene for a few hours already banded together and spoke in low tones among themselves. They deliberated on just what to do about the afflicted building. No one had ever seen anything like it. At first they sprayed the building with a bit of water, but it was a feeble attempt and did nothing. Plus, it was raining ... *hard*.

How could someone fight a fire that was unaffected by water?

Still, the purple flames raged. Not to mention the criss-cross of fluorescent lightning bolts shooting across the interior walls. No one wanted to touch the building for fear of getting shocked.

Meanwhile, the smoke continued to rise thick and proud in a tall funnel until, almost a mile above the ground, it rolled over itself and expanded into a billowing cap the exact shape of an umbrella.

"How did this happen?!" A local Meerkat, whose house was nearby, demanded as he approached the scene.

A few of the Fire Marshals glanced up but said nothing.

But Ms. Whakdak immediately came to attention. And though the kind and placating Fire Marshal attending to her rocky emotions was midsentence ("Oh yes, I *very* much understand how *upsetting* this must be . . . especially because of the *importance* of the work you do with the youth of this community, and . . . how *well* you do it . . ."), she rocked up onto her strong hind jumpers and her head could suddenly be seen peering above the crowd.

"This is another one of Laoch's experiments!" she cried bitterly to whomever would listen.

The Meerkat who asked the question looked about, wondering fearfully who this Laoch fellow might be. For he was an unsociable old Being who avoided youngsters as much as possible.

"It'll be alright, friend, it's all getting sorted. You have nothing to worry about." Laoch's father appeared quickly and took the elderly and much confused Meerkat by the shoulder. "Now now, the Marshals have it under control, and this crowd . . . well, they're just a bunch of busybodies."

Some adjacent onlookers perked up at this apparent insult, so Laoch's father winked at them as if to say he didn't really mean it. He was well liked in the community for just this reason.

"Now what do you say about stopping off at the pub with me for a small nip? Awful cold out here in this rain—"

And so the two of them straggled off.

The throng that had gathered around the scene—including many of the students' parents—had been standing about for hours, but as Laoch's father and the elderly Meerkat disappeared back into town, they too began to loosen up. The Lizards seemed to realize how cold they really were, and gazed almost catatonically through watery eyes. Meerkats shook their coats, sending water flying, and remembered they hadn't yet eaten supper. Hoppers hopped off one by one to find solace near a warm hearth.

And as they departed the strangely beautiful sight—the schoolhouse engulfed in streaking light and purple flames, glowing within the bluster of the storm—many also sighed a sigh of relief. The summers in the Southern Hills were always hot and dry, but never as hot and dry as this year. A severe drought had plagued the area for the past two months. This made the rain doubly welcome.

Without the rain, the summer crops would have failed.

A short while later, Laoch's father trekked home on muddy streets from the local pub where he had shared a tale or two with the old Meerkat. He began to feel his blood slow, and anticipated with relief the warm fire his wife had undoubtedly lit in their large stone fireplace. Tomorrow he'd have a long day in the fields to see how his crops fared, finally receiving the water they so desperately needed.

Yes, tonight he would let his son hide out in the woods with his troublemaker friends. He chuckled at the thought of them shivering in their tree house. It was a beautiful structure, to be sure. And the burning schoolhouse was nothing to scoff at. But Laoch needed to learn how to channel his ideas. And tomorrow he would fetch his son from his tree house hideout and give him something very long and arduous to channel his energy toward, make no mistake.

Meanwhile, the Fire Marshals shook their heads, not without a slight sense of awe that such a young fellow had managed to create a fire that even they could not put out.

"Are you sure it wasn't . . . *them*," some of the townspeople had whispered about the ordeal. A few Fire Marshals had been thinking the same thing but kept it to themselves.

"How could a *boy* do this?!" someone else had said before being hushed. "Doesn't it seem like the work of—"

But that was all speculation. Ms. Whakdak was extremely clear about whom she believed to be responsible.

By sundown it was ascertained that the flames were rather contained, or at least showed no sign of spreading beyond the schoolhouse itself. And so, there being nothing else to do, the Fire Marshals eventually departed from the scene.

Shortly after, the flames did, finally, die out. And left in the darkness of the rainy night, the schoolhouse stood largely unharmed, save the melted windows and a slightly crooked chimney protruding from the woodstove.

Chapter 4

WHEN THE WATER BOILS, THE WORLD TOILS

The next morning, not far from the Central Column in the city of Utomia, Dosha's kettle was about to let out a high, thin whistle. The old Hopper hunched over a table in the center of the room, his back resembling a boulder—covered, as it was, in lichens, dirt, skin shadows, and small insects. The skin of the reverently aged.

The table in front of him was almost completely covered with glass beakers and tubing of all shapes and sizes. He fiddled with the instruments absentmindedly, mumbling non-sensical words to no one but himself, for he was alone.

"Even beetle, teenie one . . . Rope the right-o . . . oats and snow crow—"

He began humming in between phrases, and soon found himself outright singing as he worked.

"When the WATCH strikes CLO-VER, a Being's gotta ASK! . . . A beautiful day, the BUB-BLE of a day . . . a RAIN-BOW of colors . . . a nasty old RASH!"

Above him, a window overlooking the city was cracked open, letting in the cool morning air. On the sill sat all number of potted plants (gifts from his neighbor, who tended them as well): some bursting with aspirational succulents, others with spiky cacti, and still others with fragrant flowers whose velvety petals seemed *just* past their prime. A bee bounced happily from bloom to bloom, and the very first rays of grayish sunlight illuminated the feathers of a large bluebird tucked between the pots.

Dosha did not so much as raise an eye from the beakers in front of him as the kettle whined. An arm-like apparatus made of bamboo swiveled toward the stove. Simultaneously, a heavy disc affixed to a rope pulley lowered and turned the burner's small knob, the blue flame disappearing with a small *puff.* The swinging arm, meanwhile, looped effortlessly though the kettle's handle, tipping it ever-so-gently to pour the piping-hot contents into a large, round mug.

A second arm appeared, attached to a track system on the ceiling. It glided toward a crowded pantry, snatched a tea bag from a jar, then tracked its way back to the stove where it simply dropped the bag into the mug. At this point, Dosha swiveled around and said (to no one in particular):

"I believe I smell some tea!"

Just then the front door burst open. A young Tree Frog with round spectacles and a long hooded robe hopped in.

"Frederick! You're late . . . as usual." Dosha's resonant voice bore no croaks.

"Good morning, Sir," Freddie chirped, "Fine morning—"

"Fine indeed if you were not late—"

"But I'm *not* late, Sir, I'm early—"

"Very well, very well, late is as late does, well, what are you doing just standing around there, fetch me my tea, for goodness sake it's probably cold already!"

As Dosha spoke he waddled to the other side of the room with his cane, though he didn't lean on it once (this being only one of the many idiosyncrasies that confounded dear Freddie). He began to gather various bottles of liquid and crystalline powders into his fronties, which managed to handle the delicate wares despite being knotty and gnarled as old tree branches. Freddie, meanwhile, hopped lithely to the stove and wrapped his sticky fingers around the mug of freshly poured tea, only to yank them back at once.

"*OUCH!*" he cried, wringing his delicate wrists. "It's burning hot!"

"Quite right, quite right, it was only just made," Dosha replied as he shuffled equipment on the long laboratory table.

Freddie blew on his singed fingers (convinced they were turning red, even though he only had the capability to turn yellow, and only under extremely emotional circumstances), cursing the old Toad for his scatterbrained ways. "Why can't you just get your own tea," he muttered under his breath.

Dosha picked up his mug with nary a startle and inhaled the sweet steam.

"When the water boils, the world toils, my dear boy. Have you any idea what that means?" Dosha's eyes twinkled. "Now *do* stop loitering and get the equipment ready for today's work. As usual we have *very* serious matters to attend to." He took a small nip of the drink and—satisfied that it was sufficiently cooled—followed it with a hearty gulp.

Freddie, appearing meeker and greener by the moment, ducked his head. Small but distinct yellow dots were slowly materializing on his otherwise bright green back (a sure sign of exhaustion and nerves). Dosha noticed them emerge from underneath the boy's cloak.

"No need to worry, Frederick, I will not replace you today. I *would* replace you, of course, for your tardiness, however—"

"But I'm *early*!"

"As I was saying, I will not replace you today because we are already running far behind schedule and finding another apprentice at this time of day"—as he spoke, the clock above the stove struck five a.m.—"would be nearly impossible as I'm sure every other suitable half-wit has most likely been dutifully employed under the tutelage of another great thinker, or, well, *someone*, I suppose, for at least a half hour already. . . .

"However, tomorrow you may find yourself out of a position depending on how things go with the growth crystal today, as there is *so* much to do and so *little* time in which to do it! Ha! Well hurry up now, I've laid out all the components, why don't you have a go at it and we'll see if we blow ourselves up—" And on and on, while poor Freddie hastily assembled a jumbled system of beakers and stands on the table, pouring powders and elixirs from various flasks into smaller vials and glass tubes.

It wasn't that Freddie was a slouch. He was, in fact, a far better fit than most of Dosha's other assistants. Having aspired to become an inventor ever since he was in primary school in the Northeastern Woodlands, Freddie was now extremely proud to know that he'd been the one and only non-Utomian apprentice Dosha had ever selected in his nearly 250-year career (for he was, indeed, the oldest living Toad on record, or so rumor had it). So Freddie strove hard to live up to the position.

It was also an honor for Freddie's family, who—back in the Northeastern Woodlands—often bragged to their friends and neighbors about their son's "important business in the city," and his "brilliant mind."

The fact of the matter was, however, that Freddie was merely polite enough to let Dosha blow them both up a few times here and there without getting angry at the old coot—or quitting like the others, most of whom only lasted a few weeks in the lab (at best). Despite Dosha's genius, his bizarre conviviality, his innovative approach, Freddie had also come to learn that the old inventor was a preeminently lazy Being. Known in the past to hire any old riffraff off the street, he almost never ventured farther than one block from his house for *anything*—including hiring an assistant.

But of course he never admitted to his sloth. "I value interest over formal training," he told Freddie once. "As long as someone wants to work, I'll find work for them to do."

Luckily for Dosha, Freddie's interest—and patience—had sustained for a few months already. Not only that: between near-death catastrophes, Freddie had indeed helped Dosha make quite a bit of progress in his research (though he had yet to clue the eager young Frog in on what the research was, in fact, for).

And while Dosha's overall contentment with the work they were doing together boded well for the relationship in general, this particular morning the stage had been set for a horrible accident to occur.

As Freddie hurriedly set up the experiment, Dosha silently sipped his tea, noting some timidity in the poor boy's movements that simply wouldn't do.

"How goes it, son?" he croaked, and Freddie jumped.

For the observant young Tree Frog had *just* noticed that the salt compound in the last receptacle (into which a highly unstable liquid would, at this point, be momentarily dispensed) was not a salt compound at all, but rather a granular version of a hybrid vanishing crystal they had developed a few weeks prior. And this was very bad indeed.

"Sir, it's almost finished, except there seems to be—"

"Very good, I knew you'd come in handy some way or another today, now stand back, I'll start the procedure—"

"But Sir! I'm *not* finished! And I think you've got the wrong substrate in the second receptacle, there's—"

"Right, as you were, though you might stand back because you never know what's going to happen, *hee-hee*, but here we go!"

And with that, Dosha, now off at one end of the long table, threw a pinch of crystalline dust into a large container of clear liquid.

Freddie, at the opposite end of the table, looked terrified. Both watched as the liquid-dust combination produced a *poof* of white steam that was immediately captured in an inverted glass funnel above the container. Dosha's mouth fell open ever-so-slightly, while Freddie's eyes bulged even farther from his shiny forehead.

The steam in the funnel quickly traveled through three loops in a long glass tube, turning from white to yellow to green, then filled a large beaker containing a translucent rose-colored crystal at the bottom. The green steam condensed into a light green liquid, which began dripping and then trickling *down down down down down*, out of a dropper at the other end and into receptacle number two.

All of this happened in a matter of moments, and right before the final drip dropped, Freddie leapt back as quickly as he could, yelling something that sounded to Dosha like *"Nooooooo"* (though he couldn't quite be sure).

"See, nothing to be afraid of—it's working perfectly," Dosha observed.

From behind the stove, Freddie glanced at the table. Dosha was right. Nothing was happening. The green liquid was seemingly binding with the particulate, which is what they wanted to happen.

"I thought it would—"

"Never mind what you *thought* it would do, son, but rather, start taking some notes on what it's *doing*."

Frederick snatched his notebook from a desk and approached the table. *The new compound seems to be stable and . . .* he began to write when suddenly and unwittingly he was blown onto his back with incredible force, his cloak ripped from his body and his ears temporarily deafened.

Dosha closed his eyes as a puff of red smoke pummeled his face and body. Glass shards flew every which way, tinkling against the other instruments and containers, the walls, and the floor.

The room was filled with a thick red cloud as Freddie (his eyes squeezed shut) crawled along the floor (very carefully so as not to cut himself on the shards), all the way to the door. He flung it open and the smoke billowed out as quickly as it had appeared.

"Frederick!" Dosha's voice called (for Freddie was still down on his hands and knees). "You *must* be more careful with the setup, you could have blown yourself up—"

"Sir," he called back, sputtering, *"th-the-the s-s-s-s-substrate, the wr-wrong, re-re-receptacle two, un-st-stable c-c-compounds—"*

"Now, now, don't blame yourself! It was a horrible mistake that you made, but we're quite alright. But before we go any further, I'll have you clean up all the glass. Cleanliness is next to—"

Freddie glanced around the floor, but there was no broken glass to be seen.

"It's invisible, of course," Dosha continued, "because of the invisibility crystal particulate in receptacle two. So yes, don't cut yourself, but well, you see, you will have to feel around to find all the pieces. Just follow your nose and you should be *fine*, good chap, just *grand*, indeed, I may make some more tea and retire to my study"—which was merely an old leather chair surrounded by three overstuffed bookcases—"while you fix up the shop!"

He gingerly hopped to his well-worn seat, settled in, then pulled a lever hidden beneath the right arm. Soon a metal disc rose up on its pulley in front of the stove, flipped on the gas, and the water was set to boil once more.

Meanwhile, Freddie stood rather still, too frightened to walk lest he crunch splintered glass into the bottoms of his thin-skinned toes. He took one last look at Dosha, the genius he'd come to learn from these past months, and decided he'd take his chances with an inventor of lesser repute. The door was still open from when he'd let out the smoke, so, mustering all of his strength, he crouched and then leapt farther than perhaps he'd ever leapt before (in order to avoid the glass-ridden floor), straight out into the narrow, quiet morning streets of Utomia.

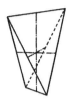

Chapter 5
A MOST PECULIAR CLOUD

D osha promptly dozed off as soon as he sat down, and even slept through the whine of his tea kettle (which was, of course, poured by his Pouring Arm). At six a.m. he was still asleep when another visitor happened upon his workshop.

Mama Meerkat poked her round, cheery face into the door and surveyed the scene.

An explosion had taken place. That much was clear.

She smiled to herself, as this was not a rare way to find the old Toad. And it was not hard to see that even his most patient apprentice had finally run off after the morning's mishap.

She stepped into the room and immediately felt the hard crunch of glass beneath her boot.

Another step. Another crunch. Step. Crunch. Step. Crunch. She glanced at the floor, but saw nothing but smooth floorboard.

Satisfied that she had taken inventory of the situation, she crunched her way back through the doorway and disappeared for only a matter of minutes (indeed, she lived just next door), before returning with ten small Meerkat kits in tow, all of them carrying brooms and buckets and wearing small sturdy boots.

"Careful now, quiet now," she whispered, and the kits went to work. The sweet young things took to sweeping the invisible shards into piles, then into buckets, then lugged them all right out the door again.

"You know where to put it! And no messing about!" she called quietly after, and was met with a round of high-pitched *"Yes, Mama"*s.

And just like that, order was restored.

Mama Meerkat, dressed as usual in a bright floral apron and matching cap (both covered with the residue of such things as meat pies and pastry flour), gracefully whisked over to the counter where one of the arms on Dosha's contraptions had gone awry (again, not an uncommon occurrence). It was repeatedly slapping a sack of flour, producing small white puffs with each slap. She twisted a knob on the wall and the arm fell still. Then she took a tea bag from the jar and set it in the water (dipping a paw in first to check if it was still hot enough to steep), poured in just a dab of honey, and carried the steaming drink over to the sleeping Toad.

"Why good morning, Mr. Dosha!"

His eyes popped open at once, his body stiffly stretching in his chair as he cleared his throat.

"Oh good *morning*, Mama Meerkat," he replied, bowing his head to her as he took the tea from her hands. "Did Frederick let you in?"

"No, he seems to have . . . stepped out," she replied, and winked at him. "It seems you've lost another one."

"I see, I see," he murmured. "Yet another—"

"Of course he *might* come back," she offered encouragingly.

"Oh that dear boy could never set up an experiment correctly—"

"You'll find another one—"

"Quite, quite."

"Invisible glass?"

"If one cannot see something, my dear, it must not exist!" he retorted. They locked eyes for a moment and laughed.

Mama Meerkat shuffled her feet.

"Would you mind—" she began, but before she could finish saying that she might, well, like to sit down, Dosha's hind jumper intuitively snagged a small wooden stool from across the way and expertly positioned it behind her.

"Why thank you!"

"I live for your comfort," Dosha replied, and Mama Meerkat blushed.

For a few minutes, the two just sat there while he sipped his tea.

"Mr. Dosha?"

"Yes, Mama Meerkat? By the way, this tea is tremendous."

"Oh good!"

"Did you put honey in it?"

"Just a bit."

"Perfection, Mama Meerkat, perfection."

They passed again and Mama Meerkat glanced over at the window. The sun was starting to rise higher in the sky, its sharp rays diluted by the Water Shield.

But she could still see it.

The dark cloud just over the horizon.

Her eyebrows knit together.

"So the reason I'm here—"

"So pleasant a visit—"

"Of course, Mr. Dosha, of course. But you see, I was up quite early this morning because, well, I have to tell you, I heard something of an — an — an explosion, you see. Yes, I believe it was *that* that woke me—"

"*Hmmm*, strange. Go on."

"And I looked out the window, and saw something unusual."

"Continue."

"A cloud."

"A cloud?"

"Yes. A . . . a most peculiar cloud."

There was a pause.

Mama Meerkat moved one of her graceful lower paws over the rutted floorboard.

Dosha tapped his foot.

"A storm cloud, you say?"

"I don't think so, though it might be. But no, no, I really don't think so."

"Hmmm."

"Mm-hmm."

"A large cloud, you say?"

"Yes, quite large."

"Hmmm."

"Yes."

Another pause.

"And what color was the cloud?"

Mama Meerkat bit her lip, revealing a row of straight, glistening-white, and very sharp-looking teeth. She patted her apron into her lap.

"Well, Mr. Dosha, it was purple."

"Purple! You don't say!"

"Yes, purple. It's still there. I can see it now."

She gestured toward the window. Dosha rose and reached to place his cup on a side table. Instinctively, Mama Meerkat slid a saucer underneath just as he set it down.

They moved in tandem to the window and had a look.

She was, of course, correct.

There, in the far distance, just over the horizon in the direction of the Southern Hills, was a tall mushroom-shaped cloud. It was deep purple.

The two stared for a few minutes, somewhat lost in their own thoughts. The cloud was enough of a preoccupation that they could also pretend that their toes were not slightly touching.

(Though they were.)

"We'll mobilize, of course," she said finally.

"When the water boils, the world toils," Dosha murmured, and she clucked her tongue at him and laughed. He winked at her and added, "I think you know what I mean."

"Of course, Mr. Dosha, I always know." She blushed again in that hidden Meerkat way, and stepped toward the door. "Shall you be joining us for dinner tonight?" she asked, as usual.

"It would be a pleasure and an honor," he replied, as usual. And then she left.

Dosha, still at the window, turned back to the horizon. An almost imperceptible smile crept over his face.

He reached his burnt by brown fingers into the pocket of the slouchy houndstooth knickerbockers he always wore, and placed a miniature stone obelisk on the windowsill.

A bluebird immediately untucked itself from underneath the eave of the sill and perched next to the object. Then, with no more than a bob of its little blue head, the bird grasped the obelisk in its delicate talons and swooped away.

Chapter 6

THE KING'S LAIR

"But Olc is in the Fásachlands!" Gustar whispered forcefully. A large Iguana and great warrior, he paced imposingly across the room, his metal armor clanking with each step.

Spreag, a Meerkat in the prime of his middle years, adjusted his spectacles and turned away from the window to watch the others debate.

"We don't know that for certain," Faichill replied, the most cautious of the King's Consuls. "Who was the last to see him there, and when?" Being a Toad (and an old dusty one at that), Faichill preferred most times to wait and see, rather than act impulsively.

"Something feels different about this to me," Ciall, a large red-and-yellow Woodland Frog, chimed in. His strength was his intuition, and the King valued his insight greatly.

Spreag was about to jump into the conversation when without warning something smashed on the glass behind his head. The agile Meerkat spun around to see a bluebird hovering midair, a stone gripped in its talons.

"Yah, yah, be gone!" Spreag yelled, waving his paw. For they were in the direst of meetings and could not be disturbed. It would return if the message was important enough.

"Silly bird," he muttered, returning to the others. "It almost broke the glass."

"Strange," Ciall added quietly.

No one else paid the bird much heed.

"Let's not lose focus!" Gustar cried, clearly the most agitated of them all. He appeared ready to go into battle that very moment. His huge mohawk spikes were fully extended, and his footsteps echoed across the stone floor.

Spreag snapped his fingers, thinking out loud. "Let's say Olc *is* in the Fás. What else could cause smoke like this, then?"

He continued snapping as if it might spur an answer, and began pacing in tandem with Gustar, one on either side of a shadowed figure sitting soundlessly in the center of the room.

As their pacing continued, the figure, swathed in blankets, made not a peep.

"Has there ever been anything *other* than a crystal that could create colored smoke?" As he spoke, Spreag again adjusted his glasses, each lens shaped like a tiny hexagon.

"No, not that I've seen," Ciall answered. The others shook their heads, and Gustar rapped the tip of his sword on the floor, commanding attention.

"So we know there is a crystal involved," he began, "but in order for it to activate, it needs a source. And the only known source is the *Máthair*—" He broke off, gesturing toward the ceiling of the room.

Above them, through brick and stone, the cogs of the Water Clock turned in slow motion and beat forth another moment or two. Deep within this mechanism lay—as it had for almost two millennia—the entity to which he referred, the *Máthair*.

"But Gustar," Spreag interjected, "you're already forgetting that there *is* another source. The piece of the *Máthair* that's around Olc's neck." He hesitated. "The *Scath Máthair*."

"Don't call it that!" Gustar barked. "I honor no name bequeathed by that monster—"

The shadowed figure in the chair raised a frail hand from within the blankets, and Gustar quieted.

The hand retracted.

"Maybe there's a third! Wouldn't that be *ter-ri-ble*!" Faichill exclaimed. His voice crescendoed into a high-pitched croak (as sometimes happened), and the others looked at the floor in embarrassment.

"There most certainly is not," Spreag noted. "There has never been a third. There has never even been a second. And Olc would never diminish the power of his by dividing it. So that's . . ." he began, but then trailed off, gently scratching his claws over the windowsill and gazing out toward the Southern Hills.

There, over the horizon, was an ever-growing purple cloud. *Smoke*, his wife had whispered to him earlier that morning, just before he roused the others and gathered them in the King's chamber. Their leader was too ill to meet elsewhere.

"It *is* a possibility—" Gustar started, but Spreag cut him off.

"We know what you think *may* have happened. And again, I must maintain: it would have been impossible for you to splinter his crystal."

They'd had this conversation before, and Spreag was sick of it.

"None of you were there," Gustar replied, his eyes clear, his voice low. He was the only Being who had ever succeeded in injuring Olc and lived to tell the tale.

Faichill let out a nervous laugh. "Let's move on—" he offered, but Gustar wouldn't hear of it.

"I know what I heard."

"Yes, we all know!" Spreag hissed, his teeth bared.

It was rare for the Consuls to fight, but no one had ever seen purple smoke outside of Utomia before.

"And if it *were* true that you chipped the crystal," Spreag continued, his voice rising as he spoke, "then he would have scoured the countryside. That's why I think it was never splintered to begin with. And even if it *was*, he would have recovered the shard by now. There's no question of that."

"There is always a question," a deep, broken voice issued forth. All of them stopped. The shadowed figure had finally spoken. He coughed, and his whole body shook.

"My Lord, but doesn't it seem unlikely?" Spreag continued.

"While it may be unlikely, it is not impossible. Nothing is impossible, as you very well know." The King paused, and coughed again. "When two young Lizards were out playing in the plains above Tradail, what were the chances they would come across what they did? What were the chances they would have interest enough to uncover that dirty mound of rock, and then the strange compulsion to bring it back to the village? Neither of them knew what was to come."

The others nodded. Gustar and Spreag stopped pacing and eyed each other over the King's head.

"No one knew. No one ever could have known." He paused, taking another deep breath. "This is the truth of our lives. We've all been crafted by what came from their discovery . . . from what they *did* with that discovery. This *time*! This time we all have. Who would have thought that a sand-covered rock might give us all so much time? And now—look at us. We differentiate. Those who are here, those who are Outside. And this we feel in our bones, something that we like to call *fate*. Ha!" He laughed, the blankets around him shaking. A glass of water on the table next to him rattled. "There is no such thing. Even as a young Being, when my father, the venerable ninth King of Utomia and a *good* King, a good *Being*—when he told me this, I did not believe him. I felt I would be great as he was great, and that there was a natural order to our lives here, and to the lives of those outside the Shield. And I was wrong. There is no order. There is no reason to be within the Shield or on the Outside. We just *are*."

The Consuls looked at each other uneasily. They had heard the King speak like this only recently. They did not enjoy (nor understand) his references to the meaninglessness of the Shield. He had been coughing with more frequency as well, and with more force. The healers had advised that he stay in his chamber and rest. This he did, under strict supervision, but the Consuls feared that this was, somehow, not good for his mind. Or else that it was going altogether, and what they all feared most might actually come to pass.

"It's as if the world has become crazy," he went on. Spreag stalked off again to watch the smoke cloud through the window, and Gustar resumed his pacing. Ciall and Faichill lowered their eyes. "Every Being has its specific place. You knew you were going to be a scholar"—the King pointed a crooked finger in Faichill's direction—"from the time you were a Childling. You knew you'd never leave Utomia for the Outside, that there wasn't enough time for you there."

Faichill cleared his throat. He had actually thought not infrequently in recent years that he might have been happier having lived a quiet life in the countryside, perhaps raising chickens and a few Childlings of his own. For he was unmarried and childless, and his life—though extended, of course, having spent it entirely within the city—was predominantly behind him nonetheless. But these were thoughts he would never share with anyone, and so he simply nodded and the King carried on.

"And the Meerkats of the Cascade Sea," he sputtered, "they know they are meant for sport. Sport! What is it, even? A folly on battle? There was no battle before the boys found what they did. They grew into men who created order out of things, thinking they were expanding the world. Well. The day that the Water Clock was set, the world became very small."

With that, Gustar slammed down his staff.

"King! Beg pardon, but we all know the story of which you speak—the *boys*, the *crystal*, the *powers* it bestowed, the *time* it gives us, the *Water Clock* and *this* and *that* . . . but now . . . *NOW* . . . there is *PURPLE SMOKE* rising on the horizon, and *WE MUST ACT QUICKLY*!"

The King seemed unperturbed by Gustar's outburst and gestured gently toward the window. "What I am saying, my dear sirs, is to take care in this situation. We do not know if there is another crystal like the *Máthair* that exists, or if the smoke was created by Olc, or even another Being who perchance stumbled upon a shard of Olc's crystal. But whatever the case may be, we should remain cautious in the approach. For as many boundaries as the Shield of Utomia has created for the world, it is now undoable. And it would mean the demise of many *Beings* . . . our very *way* of being . . . were the Shield to fall.

"You are right, Gustar. We must act. I trust you to lead the forces to the Southern Hills. Do not return without understanding what has happened. If you encounter Olc, I bid you much strength. He may have new crystals in his defense. Move wisely.

"Spreag, you must make sure the Wall is fortified, and send word to the Sea. We may need them.

"Ciall, the smoke is your task. Try to replicate it. Study the shape of the cloud it has formed. If this was created in the presence of a crystal that is not a part of the *Máthair*, we must know this information as soon as possible.

"Faichill, gather your intelligence. Find out everything you can about the northern towns in the Southern Hills."

"Yes, your Honor," they replied one by one, and filed out the door in matching green-and-gold vestments—the Utomian colors.

All left, that is, except for Ciall.

"There is still a great possibility that it is Olc," the Frog started, speaking in low tones. The King nodded. "But something does not feel right about that, for some reason. I have a strong sense that he is not near, that he is very far in the Fás."

"We will not know until we know."

"Yes, your Honor, until we know."

"I need you to do something for me," the King added. He coughed violently, the blankets falling from his body to reveal a shriveled Lizard, gray shadows of skin rippling off bones. "You know that my time is almost out, Ciall."

"Yes, I know."

"And the populace is unaware, as my time was not made public at my Re-Setting."

"The city has no idea."

"It was not revealed to me that I should die without an heir. For when my vision came and I chose my time—" The King paused, overcome with a spasm of coughs. "When I chose my time, I could see him again."

"See who?"

"My son. My heir."

"My Lord—"

"He was in the streets—"

"But you must remember, my Lord, what happened—" Ciall insisted.

"He was laughing and looking at the sky!"

"My Lord, you have no—"

"Tell no one of my vision, Ciall."

"Of course not, my Lord."

The King drifted off for a moment, and Ciall sighed. He was not lying to the King when he said he would tell no one of their conversation, but not because he felt the need to protect the King's strange memory. Nor did he believe it had any trace of veracity whatsoever. Rather, Ciall knew he must, for as long as possible, protect all of Utomia from the knowledge that their King and Leader's mind was quickly dissolving into strange illusions.

"King, there was no way to predict what happened."

"I know the Clock does not depict all life and death, only that of the setter. And yet, that vision was so clear. So clear." He fell again into a fit of racked sputtering.

"We do not know for *certain*, I suppose—" Ciall offered, though he felt he did.

"We do not know anything for certain," the King echoed. "But in any case, we must proceed in the *best way*."

Ciall nodded.

"I'll need you to go back to the first book. The version from Athair and Olc, not Athair alone. The information we will need is in there. I need you to read it, and again, you must tell no one. It will help you find the correct memory to activate."

Ciall nodded again. He had never been asked to activate a defunct memory before. And there were scores of them: experiences, memories, information, all downloaded through old technologies and embedded deep within the infrastructure of the city itself.

"Gather others you trust to help you. They should be activated by the time the warm months are upon us."

Ciall was filled with a sense of dread.

"But it is already the first moon of the—" he began, but stopped. The King's time must be coming sooner than he had imagined. "Yes my Lord, I will do this."

"Tell no one, Ciall. There must be no knowledge of the timing of this change."

Again, he assured him: "I shall not breathe a word, my Lord."

And with that, the King rested his head against the high back of the chair and closed his eyes.

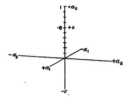

Chapter 7

WHISPERS OF THE WATER CLOCK

"*OUCH!* Watch it!"

Sty sprang from his perch overlooking the campsite after someone stomped on his wing without warning. He thought the others were still asleep.

"Oh goodness!" Leeland exclaimed, equally startled. He stumbled backward (for it was still quite dark), and as he grasped for a stronghold, managed to land his foot smack onto Sty's *other* wing.

"Do you *MIND*?!" the Bat more hissed than whispered, tucking both wings up against his body lest he be assaulted a third time.

"Sorry! Sorry! I can't see anything!" Leeland warbled, about to topple over when he finally landed a grip.

"What are you doing up? Are you feeling alright?" Sty asked. It was very early in the morning and the others snored softly.

But Leeland—who had tossed and turned all night and finally gave up on sleep altogether—didn't respond, for he had already slipped away and begun to quietly descend the tree house to the ground below.

"I'm *not* up, big mouth, but now I'm *awake*," Nudge shot back, roused by the commotion. "Thanks a whole lot—"

Laoch sat up with a jolt.

"What time is it?!" he asked, squinting as day distantly whispered forth. For a moment he felt confused—he was not at home. He'd been dreaming, but it was getting fuzzier by the moment. In the dream he was blind and his body was being pressed on all sides, and yet there was the sensation of movement. Something was not right.

Blinking, Laoch finally registered that the lump next to him was Nudge, still curled upon his bed mat. He spotted Sty, a shadow perched at the edge of the platform, keeping watch.

"Where's Leeland?" he asked, feeling for his brother.

"I don't know, maybe stepping on someone else's wings?" Sty replied dolefully, his gaze unwavering from the lookout.

Nudge giggled beneath his blanket.

Laoch sighed and lay back. If Leeland wanted to get a head start on the day, that was his problem. For this was not a day Laoch was particularly looking forward to. Still, it was hard to fall back asleep once he started thinking about what had happened at the schoolhouse. He sighed. The dim light around the boys grew brighter by the minute.

"Nudge?"

"Yeah, Sty."

"Do you think they'll come looking for us here?"

"Doubtful," Nudge muttered. He sniffed the air, then rolled over in his bunk, his stomach growling audibly. The smell of wood smoke began to waft up from the campsite below.

Laoch propped himself on an elbow and looked uneasily at his friends. The deep voice of thunder shuddered through the air as light rain fell outside their shelter.

"You *know* no one comes here," Laoch asserted. "The townspeople are idiots."

The Smelderlings, an island of forest where the boys had chosen to build their tree house, was named for the vicious vines that grew rampantly throughout. Surrounded by wheat fields on all sides—and perhaps one of the only areas of the Southern Hills *not* used for farming—the woods were shunned by most locals, who believed the vine's leaves and berries to be poisonous. To be certain, coming into contact with them could cause large boils on the skin, often resulting in thick, ugly scars. But the boys had discovered what the townspeople had not: Smelderling vines only caused harm when in direct light. Still, the others' lack of understanding kept them away, and the youngsters had (so they believed) total privacy.

"But what if they *do* come looking for us? What if we're in big trouble this time?"

"We won't be."

"You don't know that, Laoch."

Sty's words hung in the air. The boys shifted in their bunks uncomfortably, listening to another foreboding roll of thunder resound over the hills. None of them truly believed they'd go unpunished for what they'd done.

"Laoch?"

"Yeah, Nudge."

"What do you think it's like inside the Water Shield?"

He was referring, of course, to the *city*. Utomia. A topic they could talk about endlessly.

"*I* think everyone walks around all wavy-like, saying, '*COO-coo, COO-coo*—'" Nudge exclaimed in his mock-crazy voice, answering his own question.

"Oh shush up! You wouldn't know a Utomian if they hit you in your furry face," Laoch retorted impatiently. "*I* think it's better inside the Shield than . . . than any place we've ever imagined. In fact, I know it is."

"But *how* do you know?"

Sty's voice sounded very small and nervous.

"Because it moves more slowly there."

"What does?"

"*Time*, silly," Nudge murmured, his chin tucked into his chest as he groomed his fluffy chest fur.

"But how do we *know*," Sty continued. "I heard it's just a rumor. If it *was* true, wouldn't they teach us about it in school?"

"It *is* true," Laoch insisted, raising his voice. "They have technologies like we've never seen—"

"But it's an *ancient* city!"

"Doesn't matter, Sty, it's *different*. Something happened there a long time ago. Something that no one understood. I heard my father talking about it—"

"Really? When?"

"About two years ago. I was out back cleaning grain buckets when I heard Father and the postman talking. You know, Mr. Moongate . . . with the Western Winged service, or whatever it's called."

The boys nodded in agreement. Yes, they all knew who Mr. Moongate was—a well-worn Meerkat whose gray fur hung on his rakish body like a tattered cloak. He was responsible for bringing letters and other small packages between the Southern Hills and areas to the north, like the Fásachlands, the Northeastern Woodlands, the Cascade Sea, and sometimes, Utomia.

"They were whispering," Laoch continued, "but I could still hear. Mr. Moongate was trying to tell him something about the city. He was talking about the Water Clock, and he said the Shield was going to be weak soon—"

"Weak? What does *that* mean?" Sty asked.

"I don't know, that was all he said. They talked about something called the *Máthair*, and about going back to the way things used to be. Mr. Moongate said something about the ancient technologies being taken out again. And my father just kept saying *mm-hmm, mm-hmm*, like he was agreeing with him." Laoch paused for emphasis. "*Then* Mr. Moongate handed him something."

"What? How do you know?" Nudge squeaked, pulling out a few too many chest hairs in his paw. He was clearly unsettled by the conversation.

"*Because*, dummy. He said, *'Here, take this. Read the note and pass it on when the time is right.'* Then my father thanked him for coming. That was all."

"Whoa," Sty and Nudge breathed in unison.

"What does that mean?"

"I don't know—"

"What did it say?"

"I don't *know*—"

"Did you ask him?"

"Yeah, but he just said it was a letter from his cousin, and not to eavesdrop."

Nudge giggled. That sounded like Laoch's father.

"My mom said there are *ghosts* in the city," Sty whispered.

All the boys shivered.

"They aren't real!"

"She said they are!"

"What about the Shield—do you die if you touch it?"

"No stupid, why would that happen?"

"I don't know—"

"Listen!" Laoch interjected, heart pumping. "The city isn't scary. It's amazing. It's full of all the things that this place isn't, and I don't care even if there are ghosts! I'm going to live there someday."

"Sure you are," Nudge chuckled. "Maybe you can show the Utomian ghosts your *schoolhouse trick*—" Before he could finish, however, he descended into a pile of giggles on the floor (as he was prone to do when he was stressed or nervous . . . and talk of ghosts made him very nervous indeed).

"This is serious!" Laoch cried. "The things in Utomia don't even *compare* to my experiments. If Utomia didn't matter . . .

And if the things inside the city weren't extremely important . . . Then why would the Other Army still exist?"

At this, the others grew quiet.

It was not a great idea to speak of the Other Army. They passed through the Southern Hills every so often, and this was the only great hardship the Beings there faced. Usually, a few innocents were killed or simply disappeared. Most surmised that they were taken off to prison camps far, far away in places no one in the Southern Hills had ever heard of.

The last time the Other Army and its murderous leader swept through the Southern Hills, they'd made a stop in Talamh. This was within the boys' lifetime, but they rarely spoke of it. They'd all been babies then, and no one had any real memories of the invasion—only the whispered stories they'd picked up here and there from their parents or other elders.

And while no one had a good answer to Laoch's question, they all knew he was right. Something about the northern city must be very special indeed.

For the enemy of this city was the most terrible Being alive.

"Are you okay?" Sty inquired nervously. He was looking at Nudge, who had stopped laughing and was lying on the floor in a kind of stupor.

"Yeah, I'm great," Nudge replied. "Just talking from the grave."

The others chuckled.

"That's good to hear. How about you, Laoch?"

"I'm doing just fine . . . for a ghost."

A few more giggles.

"Sty? How you holding up these days?" Nudge quipped.

"Dead as a doornail, and loving it."

This made everyone laugh again, and soon they forgot their worries about armies and enemies and magical cities. For in the company of one's brothers, the evils that haunted their imaginations—real or not—seemed impossibly far away. And in this moment, perhaps no threat at all.

Chapter 8
A CRYSTAL SHARD

"**E**agruthach!" Olc roared. The great Lizard bent over to tie his boots, his ancient face obscured in shadow. Presently, a Bison lunged through the flaps of the tent. Its head tilted to the left, as always, so that his one good eye—so large and brown and almost beautifully feminine—could regard the haggard figure before him.

"Your belt," Eagruthach snorted, and placed it on the bed. Its woolly shoulders lumbered as it retreated to the corner of his master's tent.

Through the tent flaps Olc could see the deep heather of the sky. The beginnings of day. It was often overcast in that part of the Fásachlands, where the Iron Mountains met the lava fields surrounding his encampment.

"The Dragons have assembled, my Master," Eagruthach continued.

"And the Bats?"

"They are leading already."

"And the grunts?"

This, of course, meant the Bison, like Eagruthach. It was not unheard of for Olc to pit them on the front line for a slaughter while a smaller posse of Bats and Dragons advanced in counter-attack. While large and hard to kill—both good traits on the battlefield—Bison were slow to react and generally dim-witted.

The grunts did not mean much to him at all.

"They follow the Bats. There is a command," Eagruthach answered.

"Very well, fetch me my satchel."

His servant disappeared, and Olc began to move about the tent in silence, laying out his trappings on the bed.

It was always the same. A ritual of sorts. His slitted eyes moved from one object to the other—he knew their every corner and crevice, their feel and heft, how their weight hung against his body.

A helmet, crafted of the thinnest iron. Cast almost eight hundred years ago by a Skink in the Northern Plains. Killed, afterward, with one blow to the temple.

Arm shields made of moveable steel. Cut in tessellating triangular patterns to allow lateral bending. Crafted by a Dragon over two thousand years ago. His oldest piece of armor. The Dragon disappeared into a canyon in the Iron Mountains sometime later.

In the center of this morbid display was his chest shield, which he normally wore around his neck. It was designed by Olc himself with a special compartment for the *Scath Máthair*. Today was no different. The crystal swung inside its clock mechanism and was enclosed in a small pouch. The pouch itself was cut from Iguana skin—one of Athair's best men who was scalped and left for vultures to feast on somewhere in the desert.

Next was a knife, crafted by a Mage (a Toad) in the Southern Hills. Meant for ritual and otherworldly ceremony, it was called the Communicator. One of his soldiers had stolen the blade from the Toad's home at night and thrust it into the sorry fellow's own soft throat before bringing it to Olc as a gift. This was done by either a Dragon or a Bat, about one or two hundred years ago. Though it became harder and harder to recall these details. It was during the reign of the current King of Utomia—of that he was certain.

And finally, the darts, dipped thrice in a leaf mixture from the Northern Woodlands. Hidden in his hand armor and easily expelled with a flick of the wrist. The least lethal of his weapons, their serum caused something much worse. The brain softens, but the body does not die for some time. There is much wandering in the desert. There is gnashing of teeth, which also go soft. Clawing at one's own genitals. These were obtained by a Bat in the dead of night, later killed for betrayal through circumstances unconfirmed.

Olc pulled back one of the tent flaps to reveal the dismal workings of his encampment. Bison hauled supplies here and there, and a few Bats hovered in the air, hissing orders. Most were already mobilized toward the west.

He did not know his soldiers' names. They were only shapes. Temporary forms.

Whereas Olc endured.

His was the body of the ageless: weathered over two thousand years and yet never weakened. His skin was a record of this. A calendar, almost, that had no end. While the smell of Dragons was metallic, and the smell of Bats sour and biting, his was of rot. And yet his muscles remained. The skin, the claws, the spikes, the hooded neck. Olc's arms rippled as he yanked his belt taut around his hips, watching his army prepare for battle.

Meanwhile, Eagruthach lurched along the narrow paths between tents, heading for the angular walls of Creight—Olc's prison and the center of his stronghold in the Fásachlands. Inside the prison walls was a vault to which only he and Olc had the key. This was a point of pride for the deformed Bison, who was often jeered at for his loping stride and hideous face.

"Don't trip!" a voice hissed. A whirring sensation flashed past his face. Something scratchy flitted over his bad eye.

Stupid Bats, he thought, continuing on.

"What's wrong with you, forget how to walk?!" another voice jeered in his ear.

"Be careful you don't knock into a Dragon!"

His legs stumbled over something and he careened forward onto his front hooves with a groan.

"Stay away!" Eagruthach bellowed, turning his head this way and that, and scanning the air with his one good eye. His arms tensed, ready to swing. But the Bats were too quick, and all he saw was the ever-brightening gray of the morning sky.

Again, he continued on.

"Freak!" he heard then, whispered into his ear. *"Freak, freak freak—"*

But it was only the wind.

The candle in the corner flickered. Olc waited for Eagruthach to return. Not patiently, but tiredly.

Each time he closed his eyes, he felt himself slip into the void of time.

He had not slept in days. Perhaps months. There was no telling anymore. For his mind, two thousand years old, could no longer order his experiences. And so he lived as if immersed in one continuous waking dream. The past was the present was the future.

But now there was something real, something outside of himself to focus on.

A giant plume of purple smoke rising from the west.

In the earlier hours, the Bats had come calling in like rough banshees, even before the purple smoke column was visible from the ground. But by now it was unmistakable, marring the horizon. A stain.

Olc knew what it meant. His claw reached for the talisman around his neck, and he strained to feel his energy pulse. The sensation was dim. A black jewel of hate formed in the back of his eyes and he released his grip, letting the crystal swing gently against his chest.

The *Scath Máthair* was weak.

It was in a small town in the northern region of the Southern Hills where the damage was done, almost sixteen years ago.

There had been a chase.

He had taken something from Utomia.

Something they wanted back very badly.

He'd been warded off by the time he reached Talamh, which was, to his memory, a tiny farming village surrounded by vast wheat fields and fruit groves. He had stopped in a field on the outskirts of town to prepare a counterattack with his soldiers of foot and flight. Fires had begun to spring up one by one all throughout the little community, and Olc noted them like the first stars of night.

Perhaps the Beings of Talamh lit them in an effort to garner notice from the Utomians. They were, after all, a former Utomian territory. Perhaps the townspeople were afraid when Dragons and Bats clouded the sky, settling into the adjacent fields.

But very shortly after they began to shoot thin gray lines of smoke into the air, dark silhouettes had come forth. A rush of Lizards and Meerkats—still tiny over the distance of a few miles—swarmed the horizon.

Olc's leaders rang the alarm. The Lizards, he could now make out, wore thick armor and ran mostly on foot, though some galloped on the backs of ferocious-faced horses. The Meerkats came on foot, gracefully bounding in chain mail and carrying long spears and shields.

Olc's army received the warriors with just as much fury.

A bloody battle ensued. Many were slain. And the Utomians cried more fiercely than he had ever heard them cry before. For he had something precious to them, and they would stop at nothing to get it back.

And yet, as the sun set, the Utomians retreated.

This was a surprise.

This was a first.

Fools, Olc thought, and had been careless. He'd retreated as well to a stand of nearby woods until the moon rose. The ground was covered with knotted vines that made the Dragons hiss and roar. Poisonous as they were, he commanded his grunts to slash them down so that he might enter unscathed. He had something to protect.

In the meantime, while Olc planned his next move forward, one of the Utomian soldiers rose from the field of carnage.

It was a large Iguana with blue tattoos from head to foot. He had slaughtered a Dragon and feigned death. And now, as the moon crested the horizon, he crawled inside the Dragon's slain body, breathing through a small reed. The wound was covered by armor and so the Dragon, killed at dusk, appeared to be sleeping.

Olc, finally receiving word from his Bat scouts that the Utomian retreat was not in jest, mobilized by daybreak. He fondled the bundle on his back to make sure, once again, that he was still in possession of that which he had stolen. It lay lumpen and still, hidden within a thick swath of cloth. Then he and his forces struck out from underneath the cover of those spindly woods, into the golden vastness beyond.

The troops strode through a mess of fallen bodies. As they reached the edge of the battlefield, just where the soil was returning to a rich, dark color, untainted by blood, he'd passed a dead Dragon. This was rare, but not unheard of. It had fine armor, one that might come in handy for another one of his fleet. He ordered three Bats to snag it off the body when he noticed something else.

"Stop!" he hissed. It was sitting in the Dragon's hand. Something white and luminous. It could not be. Yet there it was, lying in its open, lifeless palm.

A large, glowing crystal.

Olc lunged for it, afraid that a Bat might swoop through first—there was no one that he might trust when there were crystals involved.

Then, the unthinkable happened. He could not have predicted it.

At the exact moment Olc's fingers grasped the small rock, the Iguana, still hiding inside the Dragon's body, lunged out sword first. He laid the sword straight through Olc's chest, piercing his lung.

Olc fell.

The sword was yanked out and another jab laid. This one did not penetrate but rather hit squarely on the center of his sacred pendant. Both Olc and the Iguana heard a loud crack.

This was all he remembered.

After Olc was hit, the rest of the Utomian army returned, roused by his furious yell. The Bats had failed him. In truth, just as the Iguana had hidden in the body of a fallen Dragon, the remaining Utomian troops were hiding in Talamh—in houses, barns, closets, and sheds.

And while his army fought perhaps more violently than they had in over a millennium, Olc was whisked away to the Northeastern Woodlands on a Dragon's back, so that he might be treated with plant magic.

There, in the following days, his grunts were able to heal Olc's chest. But there were a few things that were very, very wrong.

The thing he had stolen from Utomia was missing. And as Olc slept a dreamless sleep and they worked to heal his wound, those caring for him spoke fretfully.

"We cannot tell him—"

"He will know!"

"He will crush us—"

"We must lie!"

"But he will *know*—"

"Perhaps we should kill him—"

At that, the circle of dreadful Beings around his bed quieted, eyeing one another.

And somehow, like clockwork, Olc finally awoke.

As he opened his eyes, he sensed immediately that something was not right.

"Where is it?" he growled.

"It was disposed of," one of the Bats replied.

"Caught up in the battle—"

"Could not be helped—"

"Burned beyond recognition—"

And so on.

"Leave!" Olc rasped, and they filed away. Cretins, all of them. He had gone to such trouble. *And for what*, he thought bitterly.

Still. All was not lost. His troops had made many blunders, but in the end, Utomia would not be for long without that which he had taken. No matter that it was destroyed in battle— their fate would be the same. And Olc was, after all this time, a patient Being. He could wait a bit longer if in the end he got what he desired.

This gave the ancient Lizard a small measure of relief— something he had not felt for many hundreds of years, for his heart had hardened into a black pit of hatred and scorn.

Alone, Olc carefully opened the robe they had wrapped around his body. Underneath was revealed his wound, packed with leaves. And next to it, still hanging around his neck, the *Scath Máthair.*

His thick fingers grasped the mechanism, and he shut his eyes to feel it work. The normal throb he felt as the stone synchronized with his own heartbeat was now faint.

He pulled off the leather casing, which was partially shredded.

There was a very slight glow to the crystal, a perpetual luminescence. But half of it had been chipped away, one edge now jagged, and it no longer seemed fully connected to his pulse.

Since then, time had been altered. There was no mistaking this. He did not let on to anyone, and took great pains to cover it up. But he knew it was happening, little by little.

He was beginning to age.

"Here it is, Master." Eagruthach limped back into the tent, a metal box underneath his left arm. "Will I be traveling with you?"

"You think your one eye and broken leg will hold up in battle?" Olc scoffed, rising off the bed. He towered over Eagruthach. The Bison shuffled back into the shadows.

"No, Master," he replied.

"Light the other candles and be gone!"

Olc watched Eagruthach fumble with flint and a knife. Many wondered why he had spared the Bison those years ago. For he had intended to kill him, a clumsy grunt who had simply been in the wrong place at the wrong time. The Lizard had killed countless of his own before, their spilled blood leaving no impression upon him whatsoever.

But strangely, this Bison had lived. Had been mutilated, yes, but lived. And though Olc despised the awkwardness of his injured body, he took note of the Bison's tenacity. His eagerness to be spared, to continue. To please the very Being who had maimed him.

And so, Olc chose Eagruthach as his own foot servant. For—though he would never speak it aloud—the maimed beast incited feelings he imagined a father might have toward a son.

Soon the soft glow of an oil lamp filled the tent with golden light.

"Leave me be," Olc instructed, and the Bison silently slipped away.

Once alone, Olc opened the metal box. He grasped the satchel inside and let five white crystals fall into his palm.

Immediately, they began to glow, pulsing with his own heart.

So beautiful, Olc thought, overcome with a sense of power. The sight of crystals reacting to his body never ceased to amaze the primordial Lizard. It was, perhaps, one of the only pleasures still left in his life, beyond those twisted into something more perverse. His love for Eagruthach. His never-ending quest for the *Máthair*. Though even this had become more obsession than pleasure.

But seeing the crystals glimmer was something else altogether. It filled him with a feeling of connection. It mitigated the nothingness.

Olc placed each one on an appendage: one inside each boot, one inside each hand guard, one inside his helmet. Though they rubbed against his skin, he felt no pain.

He strode through the encampment. The remaining grunts, most of whom would not battle but rather take care of the day-to-day sundries for his nomadic army, hurriedly packed the rest of the supplies. Daylight was crawling ever-so-slowly into the sky, and Olc squinted. A sputtering shadow moved across his vision as a line of bats zoomed overhead, heading for the Southern Hills.

"Faster, you stupid beast!" Olc barked, kicking a Bison in the neck as it bent over to unstring a tent. The Being lurched, gagging, and another noiselessly took over its task.

"Warfore! Waylor!"

Olc crested a small knoll just outside the encampment, and as he yelled two large shadows appeared on the ground beside him. The Dragons landed with ease next to their master.

"Take me to Talamh," he ordered, climbing onto Waylor's back. They ascended into the sky, Warfore in the lead to scan for possible danger.

In the distance, a strange purple cloud rose—thin at the bottom, thick and umbrella-like at the top.

He knew what it meant.

Someone had found the shard of his *Scath Máthair*.

He gripped Waylor's neck tighter, the dark jewel of hate deepening in his chest. Underneath his armor the crystals began to hum at a high frequency, just barely perceptible as a soft whine, quivering faster and faster until they were not audible at all. Olc's pulse drew quicker still, his blood coursing with anger and fear.

He would find whoever had taken the shard. And he would kill them. For he needed that piece to stall what had begun.

They zoomed quickly through the sky, which was turning many colors with the rising of the sun—wisps of peach, yellow, and tinges of gray, blue, and periwinkle. It was a beautiful morning.

Just as the cloud grew steadily larger—the Dragons gaining ground on Talamh and the Bats now in sight ahead—Olc flexed his appendages. He tasted blood in the back of his throat and gritted his teeth, willing himself invisible while his five crystals, powered by the *Scath Máthair*, hummed their hardest and he slowly disappeared from sight.

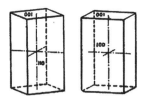

Chapter 9

THE LAND OF BROTHERS AND KINGS

eeland leaned over a ring of rocks encircling a patch of gray ash. He took a stick to it, stirring the coals. A few spindly trails of smoke issued forth, and he quickly fed them small pieces of paper bark he'd already stripped from felled branches nearby. The smoke bloomed but still there was no flame. He cupped his grippy fingers—a sure sign of Gecko lineage—around his mouth and blew.

Beside the fire ring, three freshly killed rabbits were lined up neatly, their downy necks eerily awry. Sty, the only true hunter among them, must have left them there at some point in the night.

Leeland took their limp bodies in his hands and bowed his head. Such was the tradition of the ancients. Beings that had much to be thankful for, when the land was more plentiful. But now the droughts were not uncommon; this summer's was not the first. There was less and less to go around. Less water. Less food. In turn, Beings stopped thanking the land. They relied on innovation to help them. They revered those that brought knowledge.

But Leeland had reverence for the old ways. He touched the rabbits carefully, honoring their lives cut short. *You never hurt anyone*, he thought (though there was no way to know for certain). But it just *felt* true as he held them, their bodies so silky and so lifeless. He wondered briefly if they had families, if they were young or old. And yet: no one loved rabbit stew more than Leeland. These kinds of quandaries troubled him not infrequently.

"You're like a bowl of custard!" Laoch often told him. "I've gotta toughen you up if you want to make it in this world. Only the strong prevail!" His brother would then flex his muscles, or throw Leeland over his shoulder and parade him around the house until his father finally put an end to it. The boys were twins, born minutes apart, and they loved each other fiercely. But like most brothers, their love was tempered by a healthy amount of what their parents liked to call "spirited mischief" (though truth be told, these antics were mainly instigated by just one of them in particular).

Leeland sighed and laid the rabbits back on the ground. Faint murmurs drifted from the direction of the tree house, so he knew the others would be down soon. And hungry, for they'd skipped supper last night. He grabbed the flint and struck it onto a rock, spraying sparks onto the strips of bark that had yet to take.

"Here we go, here we go now," he whispered, encouraging the fire to revive, to grow, to bring warmth and light. It was still lightly raining. It was still rather dark. Morning was just cracking over the horizon, but deep in the Smelderlings it was always shady. And save the birds of the forest, a lonely wolf haunting the woods here or there, silent as the rabbits beside him, Leeland was alone.

He hummed to himself as he worked, first laying out his instruments with precision—a small carving knife, a flat stone, a piece of thick waxed cloth they kept hidden in a tin under a rock. He then sliced the rabbits lengthwise using deep, clean cuts. He curled over his work with the focus of a surgeon, and watched the rabbits' dark blood blend into the earth below.

Crya-crya-crya-caw! a bird sounded.

Leeland lifted his gaze, facing the direction of the call.

Crya-crya-caw! it sounded again.

He hucked some of the rabbits' entrails toward the woods. In a flash, a large ebony-backed bird swooped into the clearing. It gathered the viscera in its beak without lighting down, then disappeared into the forest with nary a glance back at the little Lizard who'd so kindly shared his bounty.

This didn't bother him much, though. Leeland was accustomed to sharing everything he had.

He began to make breakfast. It was a meager stew cooked in rainwater that had collected in their camp pot, a few tender shoots growing nearby for flavor (which he knew to be edible, of course), and the rabbits—meat, skin, bones, fat, and all. His mother had taught him how to cook at a young age. "It's as much a science as an art," she touted, showing him rudimentary methods of cooking over an open fire, on spits or in iron pots and skillets. He knew that to form a hard crust on bread, he must bake it above a pan of steaming water. Or that the fermented juices of fallen fruits gathered in the groves near Sty's parents' house, usually left to rot into the ground or scavenged by small vermin, were actually quite useful to create depth in sauces and stews. Or that any meal would taste just that *bit* better when served with a sprinkle of fresh green herbs on top.

As he worked, his hums gave way to song. This was another gift from his mother. Cooking. Singing. "They go together like the night sky and the stars," she'd always said. And so as steam from the pot rose to surround his little green body, the industrious young Lizard's favorite ballad softly issued forth (for he was wary of the others hearing his tune, as they would surely tease him about the high pitch of his singing voice):

In the land of Brothers and Kings—

he dipped a whittled stick into the pot;

side by side, two Dragons without wings—

he stirred in rhythm as the wind kicked up in the branches high above him;

neither filled with royal blood
you worked your hands into the mud
in the land of Brothers and Kings!

Leeland worked his hands into the damp earth to cut the smell of blood.

In the land of Brothers and Kings
where friends unearth unearthly things
what does it take to find the truth?
bring the rock of time beneath your roof
in the land of Brothers and Kings!

The melody was sad. But Leeland smiled as he sang, for he loved these songs of the old days—tunes passed down by generations throughout the lands. His mother taught them to him when he was very young, but they originated in the Northeastern Woodlands. The tribes of Singing Tree Frogs who lived there were keepers of the world's history. Now, many of the facts had been forgotten, but the songs remained. Leeland liked to imagine he was one of the figures they described, wild and courageous and nothing like himself.

> *In the land of Brothers and Kings*
> *they set the clock until it rings*
> *don't cry, dear ones, for the water runs dry*
> *and beats against the cloudless sky*
> *in the land of Brothers and Kings!*

He stooped over the fire, now flickering nicely. Fragrant steam billowed from the pot into his face. Wood sparks crackled. He instinctively snatched the amulet hanging from his neck back into his chest, lest it be burned.

> *In the land of Brothers and Kings*
> *your time ticks off the backs of Beings—*

The sun rose higher and the dim light grew slightly less dim.

> *a bubble rises before it breaks*
> *beware the folly of old mistakes*
> *in the land of Brothers and Kings!*

He thought of how he'd stepped on Sty in the darkness. How Laoch would never do something so clumsy. The tale his father told of their birth depicted the firstborn, Laoch, as jagged, writhing, and vigorous. And Leeland, the second: diminutive and demure, with bright green skin and beautiful dark eyes. He always wanted to be held, while Laoch never stopped squirming. When they were around three years old, Laoch even carried Leeland around on his back (for he was very much the smaller of the two). Neither boy remembered this, but imagining it made Leeland smile. He continued to stir the pot.

In the land of Brothers and Kings
seal the pact that brotherhood brings

Behind him the murmur of the others' voices rose, so he quieted as he sang the last lines. He had never understood what they meant, but the words gave him a hopeful feeling. Like the rabbits' blood that drained back into the soil, returning to the land after death;

release our time and drain our blood
return the stone into the mud
in the land of Brothers and Kings!

Chapter 10
THE SOUL OF A SOLDIER

Iona slipped out of bed. The stone floor was cool beneath her calloused feet. Out the window she could see the sun cresting over the Utomian Wall. It was late for her to rise, but she had worked a Darkness Shift the night before and was not expected to return to her post until midmorning.

Still, she must not tarry. The front of her mohawk flopped down like a curly bang, and she brushed it to the side. Quickly and calmly she straightened the bed, then noted with satisfaction how nothing in her room was out of place. The desk, neat and tidy. Her closet, sparse. No frills, just a few sturdy jackets for the colder seasons, her plain military tunics, and a sash she had won from the Youth Trials. Everything in gold and green.

Along the wall leaned pieces of her Guard's armor, just where she had left them the night before. One by one, Iona donned them as she readied for the day.

Headbands. Woven brass, a gift from her father on her fourteenth birthday. Constructed specifically for her by Meerkats (the Master Metalworkers of the royal court), though the lineage of such fine armor originated many millennia ago with her own ancestors, Iguana miners of the Razor Peaks.

The bottommost band fit across her forehead and wrapped around the back, while two very thin metal panels ran up from the front, across the top of her head from side to side, then attached in the back in a diamond pattern. It was not a solid helmet, nor chain mail, but rather a small yellowish crystal in the front (by her fore brow) connected with her body as soon as it was placed on her head. Invisible shields arose between the metal bands that no arrow nor weapon might penetrate.

Next, her armbands. Solid gold. Three for each appendage. Iona slid them on with ease. They ionized her blood and served to hold other pieces of weaponry. Small pins hidden within them could be implanted in another Being should she want to track them. There were technologies built into all of her armor, and the pretty gold bands were no different.

She glanced down to make sure they were in the right position. Her plain green-and-gold tunic could not quite hide the fact that she was a female. (Most Guards, of course, were male.) Her arms, heavily tattooed with the regalia of her father and his father before that, were lithe and strong. Her neck, long. Cheekbones high with a slight scar on the left side. Her eyes, a steel blue, were large and bright, and her nose was pierced with a small golden ring.

While she had no frills about her like her younger sister, Meridian, or her mother—who had been quite glamorous in her day—Iona acknowledged that she had a different kind of beauty. The bands shone brightly against her smooth skin. No other females in her family bore the markers of the Royal Guard.

She was a warrior, just like her father. There was no mistaking this.

A prideful swell surfaced in her chest, but she quickly suppressed it and focused on the task at hand. The sun was ascending ever more quickly and she would have to report to her post soon.

Hanging over her mirror was a long chain with a golden triangular ring at the bottom. Iona looped it over her head and stared at her reflection.

It had been a present from her mother, Galánta, the day she won the Final Selection Match and began her life as a soldier. Guardsmanship was the first step, of course. Only the very best performers in the yearly Utomian Youth Brigade would qualify. In her year, there were only two. The standards were rising.

And yet. Fewer and fewer Beings wanted to be in the military as the years passed.

Some said it was because the Beings on the Outside were barbarians.

"Wouldn't that make *more* people want to join?" Iona had asked a few years ago, interjecting into her parents' conversation. "To better protect the city, were the Shield to fall?"

"Utomians are shortsighted," her father had replied. "They are afraid of what lies outside the Walls of the city. Most never leave, in fact, and so they'll never know if their opinions on the Outside are right or wrong. It is the Outside that frightens them most, not the King's death, nor the Other Army." He paused. "But it is the duty of the soldier to travel on the Outside many times in his life. He must turn away from this insular existence. He must embrace his knowledge of *both* sides."

Iona noted that her father assumed the soldiers in question were male, not female—*his* life, *he* must embrace—but kept this observation to herself. She already knew at that point there would be no other path for her. It was not a choice to become a soldier. It was, she felt, her fate.

"Why doesn't the King mandate it, then? That Utomians make pilgrimages outside the city limits a few times within their lifetime. Yearly, even. To make them more familiar with the world. To lessen their fear."

The King cannot upset the balance of things, he had explained. For if Utomians were encouraged to travel to the Outside, they might want to bring others back with them. They might see things that changed their view of their lives in Utomia. And this would threaten its very existence.

At the time, the meaning of this was not apparent to Iona. She did not understand what would be so upsetting about seeing the Outside. Soldiers traveled often beyond the Walls, and they did not upset the order of things upon returning. But she kept these further thoughts to herself. Once her father had spoken, it was not a good idea to question his words.

Sighing, Iona stared for another moment into her own eyes before releasing the ring from her fingers. She set a blank expression—*the soul of a soldier*, she was once told, *remains hidden*—and departed her room.

Her mother stood in an apron at the stove, frying fatty strips of meat and green-edged goose eggs. Grease sputtered from the pan.

Meridian and Gunn, her younger sister and brother, sat at the table, eating their morning meal before school.

"Sit, Iona. Eat something," her mother instructed.

"Did you have a nice time last night with *Rozzzzzz*?" Meridian quipped. Iona shot her a withering look and snatched a biscuit off her plate.

Roz was the other Guard-in-training who had made it through the Selection Matches with Iona a few months earlier. He was a Lizard, all Chameleon, and was just awful to work with. Iona didn't trust him, for it seemed he always had something to prove.

This made it especially hard for him to bear the fact that he had been runner-up in the final Trial.

"Roz is a chump and you know it," she mumbled, her mouth full of biscuit. Her mother placed a steaming plate in front of her, and Iona dove in vigorously. She wondered where her father was that morning, but did not miss his presence. Everyone was more relaxed when he was away. As if in response to her thoughts, however, the side door banged open.

"*Galánta,*" he barked. "Pack some food—quickly."

He reached over her mother's shoulder and plucked a piece of sizzling meat from the pan, then was gone as quickly as he'd appeared.

"Pack some food!" Gunn mimicked with mock authority, and Meridian echoed him in as deep a voice as she could muster for a Childling of twelve. Both cracked up as Iona's mother silently and adeptly packed cheese and bread and strips of meat into white canvas, then tied the parcel with string.

Iona regarded her, saying nothing.

"Can you bring this to your father?" Galánta asked.

"Yes, of course," she replied. The two women shared a small smile—so brief that Iona's siblings would not have even seen had they been watching—before Iona left, following in the footsteps of her father.

When she slipped into the stable, Gustar was busy saddling a horse and the slick crack of leather on skin and hoof on stone swelled through the room. Foot soldiers ran here and there, and her father barked orders to his Generals, who were similarly readying.

"How far from the Shield?" one of her father's favored officers asked him.

"Not very. It's in the direction of Talamh. It can't be farther than twenty or forty fields from there. Bring more than enough water—the area has been in drought."

Iona watched a few soldiers prick up their ears. Everyone had heard of Talamh.

"Do you think it's a Reaping?"

"No. I think Olc is in the Fásachlands," her father grunted, yanking down a strap so sturdily that his horse whinnied and reared.

"Now now," he whispered, smoothing his hand down its neck. *"Now now."*

Iona felt a pang of jealousy. Even such a small gesture of affection toward his horse was more than he'd ever shown her.

When he disappeared into another room, the others continued talking.

"Have you seen it yet?"

"Yes, earlier—"

"What does it look like?"

"Thin at the bottom, thick at the top—"

"It must have started sometime yesterday."

"Ustand said it was purple!"

"It is—"

Her father reemerged.

"Iona!" he commanded.

She advanced through the stable quickly and the other soldiers, mostly men, put their heads down and did not look in her direction.

"Here, Father," she said, handing him the food her mother had prepared.

He thanked her, then turned and continued his business. Iona did not leave, however.

"What has happened?"

"You haven't figured it out already? I know you've been standing over there listening for the past five minutes." His eyes gleamed as he looked her over, noting how strong she appeared in her new Guard's armor. He was not one to humor his daughter, however. "Shame to you for asking me something you already know the answer to."

With that, Iona shrank back. "Safe tomorrow," she said—a soldier's farewell—so low that he almost didn't hear her. And even if he hadn't, she wouldn't have known the better, for he showed her no response at all and instead called another order to his men.

"We leave by the Clock's next trine!" he bellowed as his daughter shrank away.

"Yes, Gustar," the soldiers replied all at once, their movements quickening, brows furrowed in concentration.

Iona tucked through an old wooden door into a hallway. *Of course he knew I was there*, she thought angrily. She was no match for him, even though stealth had been one of her strongest attributes at the Trials. She'd been able to trail and hide from any number of competitors.

"It's no wonder she developed this skill," the judges—a mixture of scholars, political consuls, scientists, artists, and military—had murmured when addressing her file. "She's been living in a shadow her whole life."

This was true. Her father was the most famed Utomian Lizard ever to live, outside of the Kingly Family. For he had injured Olc and lived to tell the tale.

Since then he'd also commanded the entire Utomian Military Forces, and with great success.

But it was not so much growing up in the shadow of her father that had helped Iona develop her talent for avoiding detection; rather, it was that she'd had to learn at a very early age how to avoid *him*. For all his success on the battlefield, Gustar had quite a temper at home, and nothing she could do seemed ever to please him.

"He yells because he is scared," her mother told her once. "Scared that someday he will fail."

But Iona did not think he would fail. Or even that he could. He seemed to out-power and outwit her at every turn, just as he did his enemies.

So be it, she thought bitterly. *I am my father's daughter.*

With that, Iona cleared all emotion from her face once again as she ducked through a series of small doors until, finally, the last one opened onto the streets of Utomia.

Chapter 11
A CRACK IN THE WALL

ona slid down the roadways noiselessly, weaving between peddlers and merchants just beginning to emerge through the city's brightly painted doors. Carts overflowing with vintage wares—spoons, cups, books, hats—clanged past her down the narrow cobblestone paths. Other wagons shuttled by, mounded with factory-grown healing crystals, preliminary-skill crystals (such as those used for turning on a light), and so forth. Now and then, one or two would loosen from a pile and scatter like pebbles. Young Meerkats—so fleet of foot—scrambled just as quickly after them, tumbling down the twisty city corridors to see who could gather them up first. Lines strung with richly dyed vestments were pulled taut between windows overhead, and on them perched all number of birds, their voices ringing sweetly with morning song. Plump Toads and luminous Frogs hopped out from their apartments, their fronties loaded precariously with books. Meerkats assembled as if out of nowhere—on ladders, on scaffolding, hoisting buckets of paint—to cram yet another building into the streetscape. Geckos leaned their heads out of upper windows, talking so quickly that others barely paid them any heed, while the designated Skink on every block made its way oh-so-slowly, broom in hand, to clear the thoroughfare of rubbish.

As Iona rounded a corner, heading from the center of the city toward the South Shield, a Chameleon hawking atop some nearby steps practically shouted in her ear:

"THE *DAILY UTOMIAN*! HOT OFF THE PRESS!"

He tossed a large green crystal in her direction. As it landed in her palm a flat light screen shot up, and upon it a scroll of words and images emerged. She scanned the headlines but her mind was elsewhere, so she stuffed it into her belt pouch for later.

Before long, she reached the edge of the city. Having been at her post for only a few weeks, she still wasn't quite used to passing through the Walls, nor the Shield. For normal citizens were not allowed past even the Inner Wall unless they were leaving the city, discouraged as this was.

"Good morning, my Lady!" quipped the graying Meerkat before her. He was an Inner Guard named Yoseph Van der Meer, and had been at the job for many years. These positions were filled by those who did well in the Youth Trials but not extraordinarily. He swiped her figure with a long, glowing sensor. It was triggered by her armor crystals, letting off a series of small beeps, but nothing else happened.

"Good morning, Yoseph Van der Meer," she replied. Unlike Beings on the Outside, Utomians had last names, though it was considered rather lowbrow if one insisted it be used.

(Which Yoseph Van der Meer did.)

"And how IS such a FINE young lady on such a SPLENDID morning?"

"Late," she retorted, pressing her palm against a stone beside the narrow doorway. The rock became translucent, revealing a hovering stream of numbers and symbols inside. Then came a flash of Iona's own face—an imprint taken when she was initiated into the Outer Guard Force—before the stone returned to its solid state and the door slid into the Wall, presenting an opening to the Between.

"Have you heard about the purple smoke?" Yoseph Van der Meer added as she brushed past him. Iona was almost a full foot taller than the Meerkat (mostly accounted for by her long neck). Her shoulder—more muscled than his, for he had grown fat and lazy at his post over the past decade—bumped him aside.

"Yes," she called, not turning back. She strode calmly but quickly down the thin corridor between the Inner and Outer Walls. Sweat beaded on her brow. Indeed, she did *not* know about the purple smoke. Unlike her father's assumption that she had put all the pieces together, the murmurings she overheard at the stable had left her uncertain, still, of what the smoke meant and why the troops were mobilizing.

Iona hurried down the last stretch of the Between, then turned left into a deep stone archway within the Outer Wall. The final Portal to the Outside. A thin sheet of water flowed from the top of the archway straight into the ground.

The Water Shield.

Iona could see through the transparent stream that Roz had beat her to their post. The other Guard, another Chameleon, stood next to him—no doubt waiting for Iona to arrive before he could go home to sleep. The Portals always required two Guards attending, no less.

She made sure not to touch the Shield. Nothing terrible would happen except that she'd bounce back from it. (Which would of course be humiliating with Roz and the other Guard right there.)

Carefully, she placed one hand on either side of the archway and closed her eyes. Immediately the stones turned transparent and two more screens, each spanning the height of her body, appeared just under the surface. Lights moved up and down at random on the scanners and finally caught her energy. The Water Shield drained in front of her, reduced to a mere line of drips, and Iona passed through easily before it reappeared moments later.

"Sorry I'm late," she mumbled.

"You're not," Roz replied. "I just wanted to get here early once I found out what had happened. Can you *believe* it?!"

Iona squinted and looked up at him. He was staring out at the plains, his hand shading his eyes from the slanted morning rays.

That's when she saw it.

Off in the distance, a tall mushroom cloud of purple smoke rose off the horizon.

She could barely speak. It was magnificent and unlike anything she'd ever seen.

"I hear it's not Olc," Roz continued, his voice dropping to a whisper. "But someone said even the Consuls aren't totally sure."

"Of course it's Olc," the other Guard replied hastily. He was older and more seasoned than Roz and Iona. "We all know that colored smoke only happens in proximity to the *Máthair*."

"Or in this case, the *Scath Máthair*—" Roz added.

"Thank you for your time, I am relieving you from Duty," Iona interrupted. She nodded at the other Guard. This was the language they had been taught to use when interchanging.

The idea was that by saying these words, there would be no question as to who was on duty and who not, should anything go wrong at the Outer Wall or security was breached. But it seemed formal and unnecessary most of the time. In recent years, many Guards had become more relaxed about protocol.

"I give you my Post, and accept my Release," the Guard replied automatically.

Roz rolled his eyes.

"See you soon," he said. They shook hands before the other Guard reentered the city in the same manner Iona had exited minutes before.

"Why do you always use that stupid line?" Roz pinched her elbow, and she squirmed away.

"Don't touch me!" she grumbled. "And it's not a stupid line. It's protocol."

"No one uses that language anymore," he continued, pacing off in the direction of the smoke. "It's going out of style."

Great way to start off the shift, Iona thought. She could see that the day ahead would probably not be much improved from the morning.

"I hope it's the biggest battle yet," Roz added. "I'd love to see it up close. Hopefully it'll move up here—"

"Don't say that, Roz," she admonished. "It's our job to *protect* the city. Why would you want the battle to be closer? That would mean the enemy could compromise—"

But he cut her off. "Correction. It's your *father's* job to protect the city. It's *your* job to sit here and relax all day in the most boring job the military has to offer."

He laughed, kicking the dust. His words cut her, but she said nothing. Yet as the dust around their legs cleared, something caught her attention. A small flower protruded from the bottom of the Wall. She knelt down, craning to see it better.

"Check it out," she called, but Roz ignored her.

The flower was small and white, with five delicate petals. It was attached to a slim woody stem that thrust out from within a very thin crack in the wall. *Odd*, Iona noted, for it was the job of certain birds to keep the Outer Wall clear of plants like these. They could root into the rock, and as they grew cause a fissure.

Iona took the bottom of the stem in her fingers, yanked, and was surprised when it would not unfasten. She tried again with more force until finally something gave. Both she and Roz heard a scraping sound as she flew backward, a huge system of tangled, dirty roots streaming from the Wall.

"What the heck!" he shouted, jumping back. "What are you doing?!"

Iona looked at what she grasped in her hands. One delicate white flower. One thin stem. And a mess of thick roots that must have been at least the size of her leg.

"What the heck," she repeated breathlessly as she examined the gaping hole it had left in the Wall. The crack was only half a foot's length in width, and perhaps the size of her fist in height, but as she squinted into the gap Iona realized it was quite deep.

Just one small flower.

And the Wall had been compromised.

Roz peered over her shoulder. "I suppose we'll have to report it," he said, sounding somewhat impressed despite himself. "That left quite a dent. You're a real powerhouse."

"Shut up, Roz," Iona murmured. She got up and pressed her hand against a stone beside the archway. Another screen appeared. "There's a crack near Portal X29, on the Outside, near the ground," she directed the screen.

"Registered," a voice chimed, seemingly from the Wall itself.

Within moments a Meerkat appeared at the inner part of the Portal, escorted by Yoseph Van der Meer.

"HE'S HERE TO FIX THE WALL!" Yoseph yelled through the Water Shield.

Iona winced.

"We *know*," she replied, "We called it in."

"VERY GOOD, VERY GOOD," he shouted back. "LET HIM THROUGH, MY LADY!"

Roz coughed, stifling laughter. Iona glared at him and released the Shield so the repairman could pass through.

"I'll just wait out there with you," Yoseph said pleasantly, following suit, but Iona put the Shield back up before he could pass.

"I'll summon you when he's finished. Go back to your post," she told him in a normal volume. There was no need to yell through the Shield, for it did not block sound.

"VERY WELL, I SHALL SPEAK WITH YOU SOON MY LADY!" he hollered back, and retreated through the Between.

"How very peculiar!" the Meerkat remarked, nudging the plant's giant root system with his toe. He didn't seem to spend much more time contemplating the whys or hows of it, however, for he'd already begun to fill the hole with cement.

Roz, flippant as usual, started to whistle in a bored sort of way. He rolled his eyes at Iona as if to say *How long is this gonna take?* and strolled away along the Wall. This wasn't allowed, but Iona was not in the mood to stop him.

Listening to the Meerkat scrape his filler into the giant crack she had unearthed, Iona let her gaze rise once again to the plume of purple smoke ahead. Strange. Foreboding. Even frightening in its stark shape.

Still, right then and there, she prayed that it might, somehow, bring about the kind of change she so desperately desired.

Chapter 12

SHADOWS IN THE SKY

"Well, I guess today's the day."

"Day for what?" Laoch asked, his voice muffled by a mouthful of rabbit stew.

"The day they catch us!" Nudge retorted. He yanked the scrap of canvas they'd been using as a napkin off Laoch's lap.

The boys sat around the campfire, devouring the meal Leeland had prepared. The thunder and rain had abated and the sun shone through the canopy above.

"Ah, they've probably forgotten all about it by now," Laoch replied. Sty and Leeland shared a knowing glance. It was certain that the townspeople had *not* forgotten about it, not even for a moment.

Still, as the boys ate, they halfheartedly joked with each other about what Whakdak might have told everyone about the ordeal at the schoolhouse, or what each boy's respective family might dole out as punishment. Soon, the stew had almost disappeared and Nudge took to licking the pot clean, much to the others' chagrin. Laoch and Leeland began to tidy the site, but Sty remained still and quiet near the edge of the clearing.

"Sty, what's eating you?" Nudge called between unseemly slurps. The Bat normally went to sleep midmorning, then started his day in the afternoon when school traditionally began. Talamh was on the Growing Schedule, which allowed farmers' children to work with their families in the daytime before attending to their studies. "You asleep already?"

Sty didn't reply. He merely blinked, then stared off into the forest.

"Sty?"

Still no reply.

"He must have really liked your stew, Leeland. I think it put him into some kind of trance."

"Hopefully it'll do the same to you," Leeland replied tartly. Nudge had the stew pot on the ground in a kind of wrestling hold, his face fully submerged.

But Laoch was concerned. He drew near to the young Bat and put his hand on his shoulder.

Sty jumped back, startled.

"I . . . I sense something."

Hearing this, Leeland stopped what he was doing, and even Nudge pulled his head from the pot.

"What is it?" Laoch asked. At times nomads would wander into the Smelderlings, unaware of the vicious promise of the vines. Usually it was a lone Skink, selling useless knickknacks from faraway bazaars, or even a Chameleon (who, through local lore, the boys believed to be headhunters—though this was, of course, unconfirmed). These visitors often stayed far from the tree house, but occasionally the boys had had some . . . encounters. "Do you hear someone?"

Leeland placed his hand on the utility knife he kept strapped to his cobbling belt (though his disposition was probably too nervous to use it, were they attacked).

"I hear them coming."

"Who?"

". . ."

"Tell us!"

"They're coming from the east—"

"Who *is* it, Sty!"

He looked around at all three of them, their expectant faces turned slightly sour with annoyance.

"The Bats."

Sty's friends did not know what it was like to have what his parents called O.S.

Other Status.

But Sty knew about it all too well.

They are nocturnal! folks would whisper insinuatingly, and yet they'd gladly trade with the Kindly Bats for their bountiful fruits. Lush plums, apples, pears, and other varieties of the sweetest nectar and juice. But then someone's chicken would go missing, and again: *It must have been one of them.*

A smile to the face. An insult to the back.

And yet so many of the Bats in Talamh and the other farming communities bore it stoically. Anything was better to those that defected (or their progeny, for many families had been living in the Southern Hills for a few hundred years), than being slave to *him.*

Sty shuddered, thinking of this. But it was true. Batkind was loyal to Olc. And except for the Kindly Bats of the Southern Hills, they were, in most Beings' eyes, demons.

Still, Sty's heart beat strangely.

For as he perched there still as a corpse, he could hear something his friends could not. Not Laoch. Not Leeland. Not

Nudge. No, they could not perceive the calls of those coming. An army, in fact, swiftly approaching their small town.

It was the first time he had heard the call of the enemy. Something the Kindly Bats in the Southern Hills taught their children about in the dead of night, the burden of Batkind. To understand the opponent, and to be seen as one of them.

And yet, to be Other.

"What are they saying?!" Nudge exclaimed for the third or fourth time. "You can understand them?"

Sty closed his eyes again, feeling it out.

"They'll be here within the hour," he began slowly. "There are grunts coming by foot." He hesitated, the others hanging on his every word. "He's coming, behind them. But not far behind—a few hours at best."

"What are *grunts*?" Leeland asked fearfully.

Laoch's face went pale.

"Do you know *why* they're coming?"

Sty closed his eyes again. A minute or two passed, but the others kept quiet this time.

"Something about . . . the smoke."

"No—"

"Wait, *what*—"

"Do they think it was us?"

Sty suddenly took to the air.

"We need to go. *Now*," he said with more conviction than the others had ever heard him muster before.

Instantly everyone sprang into action.

Without so much as another thought toward straightening their campsite, or even the fact that there was a very good chance all four boys would be in some sort of major trouble once they showed their faces back in the village, the young-sters took off with gusto usually reserved for rough play or tag. In a line, they raced through the twisty trails of the Smelder-ings, knowing just which way the path turned and where to step lightly against the encroaching vines. Sty swooped low and lightning-fast above the ground, his small heart beating something fierce inside his chest. They leapt one by one over felled logs and ducked under branches until suddenly they burst out from under the dense canopy into the blinding light of what appeared to be a brilliantly sunny morning.

"Where are we going?!" Nudge yelled, keeping pace.

"Sty, where should we go?!" Leeland echoed, more out of breath than the others.

"I don't know," Sty replied, not out of breath at all, for flying was much less strenuous than running.

"Let's circle in on the edge of town and—" Laoch called, but his words stopped there, for just as the boys crested a small knoll and the town appeared above verdant fields of new wheat, he looked finally into the sky and saw something that brought him to his knees.

There, rising from the middle of Talamh, was a huge, steady plume of purple smoke. It swirled slowly and thickly into a column that reached at least a mile into the clear blue air, then fanned out at the highest reaches, creating a giant umbrella at the top.

"Look!" he yelled, pointing wildly.

Nudge let out an embarrassingly high shriek, then the boys took off running once again with even fiercer determination.

"Oh dear, oh *dear*," Leeland whimpered from behind. Sty swung up higher to get a better look at the village, which they were rapidly approaching.

"Tuck in near the baker's!" he called. "We can rest for a moment in the stable."

Within a minute or two they reached a small shelter on the outermost edge of town. It belonged to the town baker, and was really nothing more than a shed with a roof and fenced-off square where a donkey was kept. The boys filed in despite the close quarters, crouching in tufts of hay. The donkey, there also, turned its head toward them idly and switched its tail.

"We need to stay out of sight in case they're looking for us," Laoch breathed. The others nodded in agreement.

"Can you hear it?" Nudge exclaimed excitedly.

"Only Sty can hear them—"

"No, silly, the commotion. From town!"

All four held their breath, and Laoch realized that Nudge was right: there was a terrible ruckus sounding just beyond where they were huddled. The village bell had begun to ring and he could hear men's voices yelling, the rattle of carts and wagons yanked quickly over the streets, doors slamming, and women calling their children home.

"The rest of the Kindly Bats heard them too," Sty explained, periodically pausing to receive these silent messages. "They've warned everyone. The whole town is going into lockdown."

"Well at least no one will be worrying about us, *heh-heh*," Nudge added weakly.

Laoch instantly objected: "What are you talking about? This was our fault! What if they try to find us?"

"No one's talking about us—they're just trying to get inside as quickly as possible," Sty replied.

"We need to go, Laoch. I'm worried," Leeland pleaded. But he was more than worried. He was terrified. And it showed, for his bright green skin had turned quite pale.

Laoch stepped out from underneath the still manger. To be certain, he was just as frightened as his brother, but it was not his custom to show it. Because of this he often appeared braver than he was, and the others naturally followed his lead. Now was no different. All of them winced as they moved from shadow to light, and here it crossed Laoch's mind that they were silly, the lot of them. With their tree house and their experiments. Their pranks and their invincibility. In the face of danger, all of that fell away.

"Which direction?" his brother entreated, looking to him for guidance. To step first as he had always done.

This time, though, Laoch hesitated.

He was unsure.

He stared blankly at Leeland, racking his brain for the quickest and least conspicuous route through the village, when a shadow drifted lazily across his brother's face.

Laoch blinked and looked up.

He had never seen anything like it before. Never dreamed it could really exist. Or that it would look like this.

Two massive, spiky shapes moved across the sun, silhouetted for a moment before sailing onward over the town. Their blocky heads horns and their wings—ten times the span of even the largest Bat—were taut with air and tinged with talons that even from a distance appeared menacing and razor-sharp. And the tails, jagged with spikes jutting at every which angle, rippled gracefully with muscle.

"*Dragons,*" he whispered.

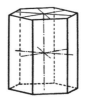

Chapter 13
HOME, BOYS, HOME!

"RUN!" Sty yelped, taking to the air.

The others scattered. Laoch yanked Leeland along by the arm, and Nudge was already off at top speed. They were all headed for the only place they could think of that might keep them safe.

Home.

"We'll have to meet up later!" Laoch called to his friends just before he and Leeland rounded a corner toward the center of the village.

"Where?" Nudge yelled back, ducking under a small gate and running straight through someone's flower patch.

"The old millhouse. Noon. There's a crack in the back door!" Sty called down to all of them before they finally dispersed, each in his own direction.

Nudge disappeared around a grain tower, moving swiftly toward his home where his mother was frantically trying to count up her brood (which was, as usual, scattered far and wide throughout the town).

Sty banked left toward the southern part of town, where his family and the other Kindly Bats lived near their fruit farms. As his body rose in the air, he was strangely unafraid. He flew expeditiously, but the thought dawned on him that his family might not even be worried about him. They were never very good at keeping track of their son, and unlike Nudge or Laoch or Leeland, he was able to come and go as he pleased, no matter the time of day or the circumstances.

As Sty approached his house—a modest wooden structure with just three rooms—something made him turn his head around and pause, hovering midair. For the strange calls and language that had reached him that morning at the tree house were back. And stronger. And closer. It caused a peculiar feeling to swell through his body from the inside out. From his very bones to the ends of his soft fur.

There, over the rooftops of Talamh, surged the commanding pillar of purple smoke. And now surrounding it were dots of black and gray, swarming like bees around a sweet stem of nectar: darting, diving, caressing the folds of weightless color that marred the perfect morning sky.

The Bats had arrived.

Something primal and hidden within him stirred. A dormant strength was awakening from a long, dreamless slumber. Their calls reverberated off his body and he closed his eyes, understanding without effort the messages they relayed.

"It's coming from down there!"

"Look at them run!"

"They think they can hide!" the Bats cackled.

And for one brief moment, instead of worrying about his friends (and everyone else in Talamh, for that matter), Sty almost smiled. The edges of his mouth curled around his sharp teeth, until suddenly he snapped out of it, shaking his head violently and darting in a beeline toward his home.

His parents—whom he discovered *were* actually worried about him—did not ask Sty about the purple smoke. Rather, while his father commenced nailing supports against the door and covering the windows with boards, his mother enveloped him in her wide, soft wings. She whispered down to him in their own language, the language of the Kindly Bats, that he was the most precious thing in the world to her, and not to worry, they would all be okay in the end.

Meanwhile, Nudge arrived at his home—a sprawling, odd-looking house his father had added bedrooms to one by one as the kits were born (six to a room, of course). Just as four of his brothers raced around a corner toward the front door, Nudge fell in line as inconspicuously as possible. Inside was a rare kind of pandemonium, for Nudge's family was almost never at home all at the same time. He smiled nervously, despite his panic, watching his father balance on a kitchen chair with a broom, swatting the kits toward their bedrooms and calling over the din: "Mother! Mother! Help me get.these damn kits organized!"

"Awww, Pop, what's the big idea?" one of his sisters complained as she was swatted toward the stairwell. "What's going on?"

"We're under attack, *that's* what's going on," he replied, already sweeping another four toward their rooms. "Now *get* in there and *stay* in there, and do *not* come out under any circumstances unless you hear from me or your mother that it's safe."

Nudge's mother, on the other hand, was standing at the front door counting as the kits rushed in. She tapped each on the head as they filed through.

"Bugle, Bonnie, Rolf, Simon, Lacer, Hettie ... oh, *dear* ... eighteen, nineteen, no wait, now we're at twenty-*one*, and there's Pudge, Henry, Hobble, Nudge, Randy—" As she stammered, trying to account for everyone, Nudge scurried into the mayhem. He ducked his head, attempting to sneak to his room undetected, when he felt a firm grip on the nape of his neck and was yanked clean off the ground.

"And where have *you* been, may I ask?"

His mother's eyes were black as two beady coals amid the graying whiskers of her laugh-worn face. Her arm, deceivingly strong, suspended him in midair.

"I was with Pudge—"

Nudge wiggled his legs, trying to get free.

"Father, look who I found here, trying to sneak in—"

"Ahhhh, so *there* he is!" his father exclaimed with mock surprise. "We've been *wondering* what had happened to you!"

"N-n-*nothing* happened to me!" Nudge protested. Luckily, at that moment another string of siblings ran through the door. His mother shot him a grim look, adding "*I'll deal with you later*" before dropping him and resuming her count. His father continued to bat the kits toward their bedrooms, from which—despite the dire circumstances and the possible, and in fact *probable* impending danger—came indelible shrieks and squeals of delight, fighting, bangs and bops, and of course, lots of contagious giggling. Nudge scooted off, hoping his parents would have their hands too full with the lot of them to bother with him for a few days, as long as he stayed out of their fur.

Laoch and Leeland still had not made it home, and were tearing through the town as stealthily as possible. The other Beings who had been scrambling through the streets were mostly tucked away inside their houses already, and Talamh appeared strangely deserted. Laoch, still grasping Leeland's hand in order to stay together, led the way, jumping mid-stride over random objects left on the streets. It was as if everyone had simply dropped their goods, or whatever they were doing, and disappeared. Tools leaned against front gates, abandoned buckets half full with water sat beneath the town pumps, and bundles of bread or cheese or flowers were discarded here or there amid random papers listlessly blowing on the ground.

"Look!" Leeland squeaked, nodding toward the sky. But Laoch had already spotted the Bats swarming the smoke plume, and so redoubled their speed. He pulled his brother along with all his might until finally they reached their house. The brothers banged through the front door with a loud scuffle and almost fell over their father, who—as usual—seemed to have a sixth sense about their arrival. He opened the door from the inside just as they pummeled through it, landing both Laoch and Leeland in a pile on the floor.

"Well look who it is."

Chapter 14
EYES OF THE DEAD

As soon as the Other Army descended upon Talamh, Olc's Generals began to conduct trials in the center of the village. Citizens were brought in for questioning. Some were released. Some were not so lucky. Among them were many farmers, a few craftspeople, and a large Hopper named Ms. Whakdak, the local schoolteacher.

And it was she who was tied to a chair—amid a circle of soldiers in a small intersection not far from the smoking schoolhouse—when Olc himself arrived. Invisible under the spell of his five hidden crystals, he descended from Waylor's back. Beside him was a crowd of townspeople the Other Bats had assembled. They were penned in by a rudimentary fence one of the grunts had constructed with oiled wire.

While many of the incarcerated Beings shrank back and screamed when not one but two large Dragons landed oh so *very* close by (for Warfore was close on Waylor's tail, the two never far from each other), no one so much as blinked when the Dragons' master stepped onto the muddy ground. Nor did they see him stride past the pen and through the circle of guards to the center of the interrogation ring. Nor did they notice as he began to pace beside one very frightened Toad and one very menacing Bat.

"What do you know?!" Tider, the Bat Leader, demanded. He circled the squirming mass of Toad flesh, his breaths sharp through a row of little teeth that gleamed near her round, soft neck.

"Let me go!" she croaked, wringing her fronties and trembling.

"Stop jiggling about, you buffoon!" Tider snapped as a Bison hoofed her in the side. Huge tears rolled out of the schoolteacher's eyes.

"Please let me go—I'll tell you everything. No one else knows what happened, but *I do*! I was *there*! I know who made the purple smoke! You don't want anyone in this town except for one terrible little brat! This is all *his* fault! He tried to explode the *schoolhouse*!"

"What Kind—"

"He's a Lizard, a horrible no-good Lizard!" she sobbed.

"Where can we find him?"

"On the northern edge of the town, his family has a farm. It is a small red house with a stone wall in front—you can't miss it."

"Are they there now?"

"How should I know?! Who do you think I *am*, his mother?" she cried.

"What were they doing when the purple smoke started? Did they say anything about it to you?"

"Are you not listening to me??!!" she wailed. "He is trying to *ruin* my teaching career!"

The interrogators shook their heads.

"Take her in—" Tider ordered a few grunts nearby, and waved on three other Bison to find the Lizard boy.

"Take me in??" Ms. Whakdak screamed. "What do you mean?! I told you everything you need to know—it's all the little brat's fault you stupid beast, let me *go*—" Her croaking voice reached new pitches as she cried, and Olc, tired from the journey, snapped.

At first she started to cough. Two Bison escorted her toward the area where they were keeping detainees. But as they dragged her on, Ms. Whakdak's coughing grew more frantic, and her yells turned into groans, and then whimpers. Her eyes—at first so fiery and wild—turned dull and milky. Before they even reached the detention pen, her long jumpers were dragging behind her and her mouth lolled open, a small stream of drool dripping out the edge. The Bison threw her in the pen, and her body rolled limply on the ground. The other townspeople gathered around her.

"Ms. Whakdak!" they cried, shaking her body, waving their hands in front of her face. "Ms. Whakdak!"

But there was no response. Her eyes blinked lazily and didn't seem to register faces, words, or anything at all.

"Is she alive?" a voice sounded.

"She's still breathing—"

"But her eyes look like those of the *dead*!"

"That's what happens when you question Olc's Army," growled one of the Bison. The other detainees quieted, looking in all directions—afraid, suddenly, of the unseen.

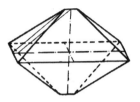

Chapter 15
A KNOCK AT THE DOOR

"Thank goodness you're finally here!" Laoch's mother cried. He helped his brother to his feet, and the two of them stood there looking at the floor. Their father calmly shut the door, his Chameleon eyes scanning them over.

"Seems you two have been up to some interesting activities of late," he said, and Laoch ducked his head.

"It wasn't supposed to happen like that, I promise. . . . We were just doing one small prank," Laoch explained, ". . . I mean *experiment* . . . and I think the rain had something to do with it, because things didn't go as planned, and I swear no one was supposed to get hurt. To be honest I don't know anything about the purple smoke at *all*, it just sort of *appeared* . . . out of nowhere, and—"

Laoch noticed that his father was only half looking at him, however, for one eye was fixed on the door. A soft thumping noise had begun in the distance, then strengthened until finally the teacups on the rack were rattling and he realized it wasn't his imagination at all, but rather the steady rhythm of very large Beings marching through the town.

"We don't have much time," his father began, taking both boys by the shoulder and leading them from the kitchen down a narrow hallway. *"Hush now,"* he whispered, then called to their mother: "Dear, please heat up the stew? We should have breakfast in a moment . . . but first I want to speak with the boys."

Hurriedly, she placed the large pot of savory duck stew on the woodstove and stoked the fire, while the men of the house gathered in a back room.

"Listen sons," their father started, sitting them down on the bed. "I don't know exactly what happened at the schoolhouse, and to tell you the truth, right now it doesn't so much matter. But *whatever* it was, it has grabbed the attention of forces in this world whom . . . whom we'd never knowingly invite to our small town. Do you understand what I'm saying?"

Laoch wasn't sure exactly what his father meant but nodded anyway.

"No one knows why . . . *he* . . . is coming. Or his army."

The boys nodded again.

"But it most likely has something to do with—"

And then Laoch understood. It was his fault. The experiment. The schoolhouse. Ms. Whakdak. The purple smoke.

He had caused it, and now the Other Army was marching on Talamh, and the whole community was in danger.

"I'm sorry Father, I'm so—" he began, buckling over, but his father pushed him back up.

"There is no *time* for that, Laoch!" he admonished. It was the first time the boys had ever heard fear in his voice, and it silenced them at once.

"I know you're sorry. But like I said . . . we can worry about the specifics later, once they're gone and everyone is accounted for. But for now . . . I need to make sure my sons are safe. Who knows what will happen?"

A loud rapping sounded on the family's front door.

"What is *th-that*?!" Leeland squeaked, his voice breaking with desperation. Their father held up a hand to silence them.

"Dear?" he called up the hallway toward the kitchen.

"There is . . . there *are* . . . some Beings at the door," their mother called back.

"Don't open it up, dear. I'll be right there," their father replied, turning back to his sons. He scooted to the end of the bed where there sat an old chest. He opened it, reaching far underneath the linens, then drew forth a small gilded disc in his palm.

"Sons. We don't have much time."

The booming knock sounded again from the front door, and Laoch heard his mother's plaintive voice call to them— *"Dear?"*—as the *rap-rap-rap* came yet again, this time with more force. Fear coursed through his veins and he noticed that his brother—small, innocent Leeland, who would never hurt a fly—was trembling. Laoch watched his father's mouth move, yet the words fell away, for his mind was filled with visions of the Dragons they'd seen earlier, their jagged shapes silhouetted against the sun. Suddenly he was sure that they were flying overhead at this very moment, right over their roof, poised, great balls of fire gathering in their throats—

"Laoch!" his father hissed. *"Listen*, son. *Listen!"*

Laoch focused his eyes and took a deep breath.

"I need to answer that door. And I need you two to crawl under the bed and stay there. Be very still. Do *not* talk, no matter what happens, and do not come out as long as there are other Beings in this house. Do you understand?"

Laoch and Leeland nodded.

"Take this, Laoch," he continued, pressing the small disc into his hand. "I can't tell you what this is. Tuck it away somewhere safe. Keep it with you always, like your amulets."

Instinctively, the brothers touched their necklaces, which were given to them by their father on their fourth birthday. "Resin," he had told them all those years ago, "and sensate wood. Passed down from generation to generation in the Northeastern Woodlands, where I am from. These will protect you and bind you as brothers for as long as you live. And you shall pass them on to your sons. But until that day, you must never take them off."

And they hadn't.

Their father then clasped their hands against their chests.

"I'm so sorry, Father—" Laoch said again. His heart beat so wildly against the amulet, he feared it would burst.

The pounding sounded again, and this time they could hear angry voices outside the door. Voices of Beings they did not recognize. Deep, gravelly voices.

"If anything happens to me, you must go north. You must leave Talamh."

"Where, Father? North to where?" Leeland whispered, on the verge of tears.

"Utomia."

The word hung for a moment in the air.

"You must bring your brother," their father continued, now looking at Laoch alone. "And the disc I just gave you. It will help you. It's a riddle, and I can't tell you more than that except it will reveal what you need in order to make things right again. To find your true path—"

"My true path? What do you mean?" Laoch interrupted. It was so strange, hearing these hushed words coming from his father's mouth. His father who had for so long pushed him toward the farming life, had tried to keep him at bay in Talamh while he dreamed endlessly of becoming a warrior, an inventor, someone with a great destiny to fulfill. And now, *Utomia*? He was *asking* Laoch to go there? It made no sense.

But there were no more words—and certainly no more time for pondering all the strange things that were happening—for Laoch's father had already nudged his sons to the floor and was scooting them under the bed.

"Remember what I told you," he whispered before making his way to the door. "Go north, Laoch, and you will find what you need."

"What about me?" Leeland whispered back, but his father was already gone.

The boys' mother was standing near the stove, calmly stirring the stew, when their father opened the door and revealed not one, not two, but three looming shapes: brown, straggly, and smelling so foul that their mother's nose wrinkled delicately. She turned her head away from their faces, which were large and hideous.

"Why hello, chaps. Can I help you?" their father asked calmly. A slight smile spread across his face. "Beautiful morning, eh?"

The first Bison poked its head through the door. "Who's in here?" it sneered, mucous flaring out of its nostrils as it exhaled violently and pawed the ground with a front hoof.

"Just me and the missus," Laoch's father replied, pointing at his wife, who waved timidly from her stance near the stovetop. "Just about to have some nice duck stew, in fact. Would you care to join us?"

"No, you imbecile!"

By then all three Bison had squeezed through the door and took up most of the space in the room, their backs reaching to the ceiling. Their shaggy manes revealed infestations of insects and all manner of excrement and filth caught in matted knots, and their tails swished menacingly.

"Where are they?" another one asked.

"Where is who?" the boys' father replied. "I've only got one wife, if that's what you mean, you naughty fellow—" he quipped, and was instantly struck by one of the intruders. He was flung back against the wall, covering his face where he'd been hit.

"Enough with the wisecracks, Lizard, you know why we're here."

"I assure you I don't, and on that note I might add that that hurt quite a bit and was highly uncalled for."

One of the Bison swung its head around into the boys' father's face and snarled, both wide, empty eyes blinking slowly. "There'll be more of that if you don't show us where they are!" he yelled. The poor Lizard farmer stumbled back against the wall again from the sheer force of its utterance as his wife let out a small gasp.

"What are you talking about?"

"The boys. The Lizard boys."

"What boys do you mean?" their mother offered weakly as another Bison batted the stirring spoon out of her hand.

"Your SONS!" another bellowed, blowing up her apron.

"Well I haven't the slightest idea of where they are," their father replied. "Let's see, what time it is now. . . ? Well, yes, they are most likely at school. They're very good boys."

This garnered him another strike, and now the Chameleon lay on the floor, struggling back to his hands and knees.

"We know what they did, Lizard," said the tallest Bison. "We just need to find them, and then we'll leave." It turned and snorted to its cohorts: "Now get to it!"

The three beasts began haphazardly batting dishes off cupboards and knocking around chairs, their bodies quite a bit too large for the space, while the boys' mother frantically scanned the room in search of some sort of weapon.

"It's alright, dear. Don't worry. I'll tell them," her husband said.

"Tell us what?!" the intruders demanded in unison.

"You're not looking for my sons. You're looking for me."

"What do you mean, fool?!"

"It was me. I did it. At the schoolhouse. I'm ... an ... inventor of sorts. It was all my doing."

His wife's eyes widened.

"That's not what they told us in town!" one of the Bison barked, its breath filling the room.

"They're wrong. I made it *seem* like it was the boys, since they wouldn't get into trouble for such an innocent prank. Oh, but it did go terribly awry, I must admit. Anyway ... it *would* be rather unseemly for a grown Lizard like myself to get up to those kinds of things. But alas, I suppose I never outgrew the tendency—"

"Do you smell any other Beings in here?" one of the Bison snarled suddenly. All three of them jutted their snouts forward and sniffed the air wildly.

"No—" another replied, for the aroma of duck stew was strong, as was their own stench, and somehow masked the smell of the young Lizards in the other room.

"Do you believe him?" one asked, turning to the others.

They thought for a moment.

"I swear it's true!" the boys' father insisted from the floor, managing finally to stand while his wife, unable to control herself anymore, began helplessly to sob and wring her slender wrists over the stove.

"We'll have to test him," another stated, turning to the Chameleon. "*Since* you think you know so much, Smarty . . . What *color* is the purple smoke?"

Laoch's father almost laughed. He had heard of the stupidity of Bison before, but did not expect it to this degree.

"It is a beautiful shade . . . like the sky before sunrise. Or the petals of an evening flower just after a rain."

Laoch's mother shot her husband a withering glance—for how could he mess about in a time like this? As a thin line of blood ran down his cheek from the blows he'd already endured, he mustered a sly smile and shrugged at her. Old habits were hard to let go of.

The Bison turned their backs and conferred, but muffled bits of their conversation bled out into the room:

". . . but is it that color BEFORE the sunrise or just AFTER?"

"If it's RAINING in the evening, will the flower still bloom?"

"Is a SHADE the same thing as a COLOR?"

One of them, the seeming leader, whipped around. "We see what you're trying to do, you unfortunate sack of scales. You can't trick us."

"We have a new question for you," another growled.

"Was the smoke meant to summon the Great One?"

"The Great Who?" asked Laoch's father, widening his eyes.

"The Monstrous One!" another clarified.

"I'm sorry, I'm not familiar—"

"OLC!" the third shouted, spraying yellow saliva about the room.

"Oh of course, well that I'm not so sure about. You see, I was there mainly to start the smoke, though once it got going I'm not responsible for who it summoned—"

"There are other ways of getting answers," a Bison sneered, stepping violently toward Laoch's mother.

"No!" his father yelled. "Please, ask me another question. I promise I will give you the information you are looking for."

The Bison's nose quivered as it glared down its arched snout at the cowering Lizards beneath it. "Tell us," it snarled, "when the smoke started."

"Why . . . I would say about twenty hours ago, approximately," Laoch's father replied quickly.

The three Bison began muttering to themselves and counting, then nodding and conferring, until finally one of them exclaimed: "Well, I believe it *was* indeed around twenty hours ago!"

"Shall we kill him?" another quickly followed, though Laoch's father failed to see the logic in this.

"No!" the boys' mother shouted.

"If you kill me, you'll never know anything about the purple smoke," the boys' father said hastily.

"Yes, I think so, let's kill them—"

"Nah," the third replied. "Remember the orders? Bring back those who started the purple smoke—"

"Right you are," said another, and before Laoch's parents could do or say another thing in their defense, they were snatched up by the Bison and whisked out the door, the large pot of stew still bubbling on the burner.

Chapter 16
NOWHERE ELSE TO GO

"We need to get out of here," Laoch whispered. The brothers slid from beneath the bed and stared noiselessly at each other, unsure of what to do next.

Suddenly there was a rap on the window. Both boys jumped, expecting to see the frightening figures behind the voices they'd heard through the walls. But it was Nudge's furry face that appeared in the glass, and a surge of relief swept through them. Leeland opened the latch and their friend climbed inside, breathless from running.

"They're all over!" he exclaimed, and Laoch shushed him severely. *"They're all over!"* he repeated, whispering. "The Other

Army. Bison. Bats. Dragons. They took over the town center! Most of them are gathered around the schoolhouse, but there are scouts on the streets too. I saw a Bison close up! It was *disgusting!*"

"Is it noon already?" Leeland asked in a daze.

"Yes! I've been waiting at the mill with Sty, but neither of you two jokers showed up so we decided to find you. What have you been doing? Where are your folks?"

A dark look went over the brothers' eyes. They glanced at each other.

"Some Bison came to the door—" Leeland began, but then broke into soft sobs, bowing his head forward in resignation.

"What are you talking about?"

At that moment, another rap came at the window, and they saw Sty peering through. Nudge quickly let him in, and Sty nestled next to Leeland, wrapping his wing around his friend's shoulder.

"I'm going to turn myself in," Laoch stated, a steely look of resolve in his eyes.

"No!" Leeland exclaimed, roused from his crying. "No, you can't! Remember what Father said!"

Sty looked on quietly but Nudge became agitated. "What are you two *talking* about?!"

"Some Bison came to the door—" Laoch began, and then recounted to his friends the whole terrible story. About the intrusion, the sound of their father's body hitting the wall, their mother's sobs, and how they were taken. About the strange things their father had told them before opening the door, and the golden disc (which Laoch then pulled from his jacket pocket).

As soon as he saw it, Nudge plucked the shiny treasure from his friend's grasp. He flipped it in the air like a coin.

"Wow," he breathed, watching it catch the light as it spun in the air. But before he could catch it, Laoch had already snatched it back.

"Don't do that!" he yelled, stuffing it safely back in his pocket.

"Where do you think they were *taken*?" Nudge asked, the seriousness of Laoch's story finally sinking in. "I mean, they were obviously after *you*"—he nodded at Laoch—"which means . . . they might be after . . . *me*."

He shuddered.

"I'm going to turn myself in. I need to get my parents back," Laoch stated again, rising toward the door. But Leeland, with uncharacteristic strength, yanked him back down by the arm.

"No, Laoch. Father said not to. He said to go north."

"You three stay here," Sty said, finally speaking up. "I'll fly out and see what's happening. Then we'll make a plan."

"You and Nudge should just go home," Laoch replied wearily. "They don't want you. Go home to your families, where it's safe."

"No way, buster," Nudge shot back. "We're in this together. We're a team, remember?"

Laoch nodded dispassionately, and Sty slipped out the window. The three remaining boys sat in silence for a bit, and before they knew it Sty had returned, his face bright with fear.

"Your parents have already been taken away," he stammered. "So there's no use in turning yourself in now. They've been taken out of Talamh."

"Is the Army gone too?"

"No. But your parents were taken east."

"Where?!" Laoch demanded. He blinked, unsure how all this could be happening so fast. Where would they have been taken?

"Creight," Sty replied. "It's a prison camp in the Fásachlands. That's all I know."

"What else did you hear?"

"The Other Bats were talking about a crystal. They said they found a few at the schoolhouse but were told they were the wrong ones—"

"Then it *can't* be us that they're looking for!" Nudge exclaimed. "Because those were the only crystals we used, right? We just need to tell them that, and they'll let everyone go!"

But even as the words came out of his mouth, he knew they were in vain. The Other Army was not known for its mercy.

And so it was decided that all four would go north, away from Talamh, and once they were out of range of the Other Army they'd decide what to do next.

"I suppose I could continue on to the Cascade Sea," Nudge offered, trying to lighten the mood. "No better time than the present to jump into the old Water Games! You know, win a few medals—" He giggled, for he was very nervous indeed.

"I've always wanted to see what the world is like outside Talamh," Sty added, mostly for moral support since that wasn't exactly true. In fact, he wasn't sure whether or not he really wanted to go, for the strange buzzing that had been running through his body since the Other Bats arrived had not ceased. He was distracted, almost enchanted by their distant calls. While his friends began to plan their journey, gathering what they could from the farmhouse, Sty quietly stared out the window.

"I don't really care what life is like outside of here," Leeland replied meekly.

But Laoch paid him no heed.

"Get your things," he instructed. They would bring only a few sacs of bread and cheese and cured rabbit meat, a few knives, extra overcoats, and each his own blanket and canister of water. Unfortunately, neither Laoch nor Leeland could locate a map, and it occurred to Leeland that perhaps his father had no use for one, having never left the Southern Hills after arriving in his youth.

Until, perhaps, now.

Leeland paused. He could not stop himself from imagining where his parents were being taken, and *how*. His lower lip began to tremble.

Laoch saw this and quickly intervened. Were Leeland to cry outright, he might follow suit.

And he of all people did not cry.

"C'mon now, snap out of it!" Laoch cuffed his brother on the shoulder. "We don't need a map anyway. I'll figure out the way—"

The others looked doubtful.

"I *will*!" he insisted. "How hard is it to walk in one direction?" He marched pointedly from one end of the room to the other. "Plus, I've practically got the map memorized!"

(This was a lie, but it spilled from his mouth effortlessly, as if to replace the fears rising in his throat.)

"Oh, because you paid *so* much attention in geography class—" Nudge quipped, trying to make a joke. No one laughed though, not even him. Indeed, everyone had ceased packing altogether. Suddenly the journey seemed unwise and even absurd—how could the four of them, inexperienced as they were, survive on their own?

Absurd to all but Laoch, that is. *If I can create purple smoke that calls Beings from the other side of the world, I can get us to Utomia,* he thought. The fact that he couldn't (or didn't) help his parents was also on his mind, but the young Lizard had an extraordinary ability to put things he didn't care to think about to the side. And while this was both troublesome and true, he decided to focus on the issue at hand: it was now dangerous for them to remain in Talamh. And he felt it was his responsibility, given all that had happened, to get them out safely.

"What's the worst thing that could happen out there?" Laoch began, trying to sort through their options. Reminding himself that emotions don't make sense, never *had* made sense, whereas logic . . . well, logic, in fact, *always did*.

"We get killed by a Dragon," Nudge replied, not skipping a beat.

"Right, okay. What else?"

"What *else*?" Leeland wailed incredulously. "What else is worse than that!" He broke into soft sobs, and Sty inched closer to his friend (as much in an effort to comfort Leeland as to comfort himself).

"Of course getting incinerated *would* be terrible . . . but I want to know what *else* could happen," Laoch continued.

No one said anything.

"Come *on* guys. Trust me. What else?"

"We could be captured," Sty offered.

"Right. Good. Captured and then what?"

"Sent to the prison camp where they brought your parents?" Nudge guessed.

"Yes! Great. What else?"

"We could be tortured—" Leeland wept.

"Good, now we're getting somewhere!" Laoch cried passionately. He paced the room, stuffing remaining supplies into their sacks. "What else?"

"We could get lost," Nudge replied. "Lost out *there*." He pointed out the window in the direction of the Great Plains.

"We could be separated," Leeland added.

"Yes!" Laoch replied, a bit of mischief in his voice. "Which might not be so bad." He yanked open a drawer and extracted a ball of twine, a flint stone, and a small hand scythe. "Come to think of it, I can't imagine spending more than a few hours at a time with you blokes."

"Or starve—"

"Very true!" He fired back, filling their water bladders from the cistern in the kitchen. "*Especially* if the food out there is as tasty as these tacker-cracks." He made a face and tossed Nudge a parcel of the hard, dry wheat crackers (which were a widely acknowledged bane of the existence of all the youth of Talamh). "What else?!"

Nudge giggled and stuffed the crackers into a bag. "We could ... we could see some new places?" he ventured, the wheels beginning to turn.

Laoch nodded him on.

"We could meet some new Beings?"

"Interesting! Go on!" Laoch bellowed, tightening the straps on their packs.

"We might learn something?" Sty added.

"Yes!" Laoch replied, tossing his brother a sweater and boots.

"We might fulfill our father's wishes," Leeland declared suddenly. Though his face was wet with tears, his eyes were resolute.

At this, Laoch stopped his hurried movements.

"You're right," he said to his brother.

"And *you're* right," to Sty.

"And *you're* right," to Nudge.

They looked to Laoch expectantly.

"*All* of these things are possibilities if we leave Talamh. But that's just it. While they *could* happen, we don't know with any certainty that they *will* happen. We can only do our best to try to get the best possible result." He stepped to the window, noting a line of grizzly looking Bats zoom over rooftops in the distance. Chills ran down his spine.

"What we *do* know, with *great* certainty, is that we are not safe here," he continued. The Other Army is here, and they are looking for"—and here his voice almost broke—". . . for *us*. And they are violent, sadistic Beings. They are worse than anything I ever imagined. They took our parents and they will take us if we stay."

He gazed toward the hind fields in the direction of the unknown. "Is there a *chance* that they will find us out on the plains? Yes. Is there a *chance* we will be killed? Or separated? Or that we will starve? Yes. But it was our father's command . . . his final request . . . that we leave Talamh. And I trust him more than anyone right now. He insisted that we go north. To Utomia."

Laoch's words cut the air with certainty and force, and the others silently accepted the task ahead. As they gathered their things, Laoch nodded and made eye contact with each one. And though he knew little of geography, and they still didn't have a map or viable plan, he also knew they didn't really have much choice in the matter . . . it was either go without a map or don't go at all, and the latter was not an option.

As twilight fell upon the land, the boys quietly snuck out the window and ducked into the tall wheat that, thankfully, was at a seasonal high despite the recent drought. It reached over their heads so that as they moved away from the farm, and the town, and the only homes they had ever known, all that could be seen was a slight rustle in the field from above, and that is all.

Under the long shadows of a setting sun, the town receding behind them was eerily silent. Every now and then the boys glanced up, and through the supple wheat berries watched the purple smoke plume, big as ever, stamped against the sky that turned slowly from blue, to pink, to coral, to green, to gray, until finally the first twinkling stars of night appeared all around.

The boys moved quickly, unsure of whether they were keeping a straight line until the brothers' family's fields ended, and they emerged into plains of thinner, scruffier grass and rolling hills.

It was at this point, though the light was quite dim, that Laoch thought he saw something in the distance. A dash of color, navy blue.

"Did you see that?" he asked disconcertedly.

"What?"

"Up ahead—"

"Nope," Nudge replied. "Just a whole lot of nothing."

Then he saw it again.

"Up there! Did you see *that*? It was blue!"

"Ah, you're just exhausted," Nudge said. "Always dreaming up something or oth—" but before he could finish, Laoch interrupted him with a loud shout.

"MR. MOONGATE!"

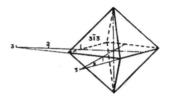

Chapter 17
BORN. LIVE. DIE.

His brother and friends watched as Laoch broke into a dead run. He was headed for the next ridge where, lo and behold, there *indeed* a figure stood. The others soon followed, and by the time they had all reached the heavily whiskered Meerkat, Laoch was already peppering him with questions.

"Where are you coming from? Where are you going? Were you in Talamh? Did you see what happened?"

"Yes yes, my boy, I know, dreadful scene, dreadful scene . . . Of course I saw the Other Army, I'm not quite *fond* of them, you see . . . yes, delivering the mail as usual—" He patted the bulging bag looped over his side, from which hundreds of letters and small parcels protruded. It crossed Laoch's mind that sending or transporting letters seemed like a futile endeavor in such dire circumstances, but nevertheless, he was grateful for Mr. Moongate's presence.

"But boys, it's not safe here. You best get home, and quickly."

"But we can't go home!" Leeland blurted.

"What do you mean you can't go home? Is there a problem?"

"No, no problem," Laoch interjected, shooting Leeland a stern look. "Actually, we're heading north . . . and I suppose we could use a little help with directions."

Mr. Moongate eyed them suspiciously.

"Well, of course I can help set you on your way," he replied finally. "But first I must ask *why* you are not home with your parents?"

Leeland looked at the ground. His lip began to quiver once more.

"My parents told me to get out," Sty lied. "They didn't want the Bats . . . I mean the *Other* Bats . . . to . . . well . . . *you know.*" Sty wasn't quite sure what he was trying to convey, but Mr. Moongate nodded knowingly.

"Quite right, quite right," he said, and Sty nodded back.

"And *my* parents told me to head north to the Water Games," Nudge added. "I've been training up, Mr. Moongate." He puffed his chest and made a muscle for the postman, who smiled in response. "Yup, no time like an invasion to get out of town and head to the Cascade Sea!"

Laoch rolled his eyes. Sometimes Nudge was just too much.

"Very good, I see. Now what about you two?"

Mr. Moongate looked sternly at Leeland and Laoch.

"Well—" Laoch began. He realized he wasn't prepared to talk about what had happened to his parents. He wasn't even really able to properly *think* about it yet. But there was no reason not to tell Mr. Moongate, as long as no one mentioned the purple smoke.

"They were kidnapped!" Leeland revealed suddenly.

"What?!" Mr. Moongate cried, his eyes narrowing. "When and by whom?"

The other boys just looked at each other, unsure of what to say.

"The Other Army . . . they just took them," Leeland continued, starting to weep.

"There, there, my boy," Mr. Moongate said, pulling the small Lizard in for a hug. "It'll be alright, just tell me what happened."

"Well—" Leeland began, while Laoch tried desperately to make eye contact. He needed to somehow communicate to Leeland that he should under *no* circumstances mention the purple smoke nor the boys' connection to it. But he didn't have to.

"They were outside, just going for some water," Leeland continued. Nudge and Sty glanced at each other. "And all of a sudden, there were these two huge ... *Bats* ... right overhead!"

Mr. Moongate nodded, rubbing Leeland's back.

"Not Bats like Sty—"

"Naturally," Mr. Moongate replied.

"But *big* Bats. Really *horrible* ones. And they came down and just snatched our parents up!" With that he broke into big, all-consuming sobs, and Mr. Moongate and the others continued to comfort him.

Laoch, on the other hand, strove to appear strong and stoic, but inside was astonished. In all their years together—as twins, no less—he'd never known Leeland to lie.

About *anything*.

Despite this, he put his arm around his brother and nodded frantically up at Mr. Moongate, trying to look convincing.

"Yes, it was horrible, Mr. Moongate," Laoch added, now rubbing Leeland's back. "We were watching from the window, because we knew it wasn't safe outside ... and we saw them get snatched up. We ran out to try to stop them somehow, but—"

"I understand, son," the old postman replied, however, he wore an expression that Laoch couldn't quite place. "So you decided to leave Talamh because your parents were kidnapped. Did you not think to call the authorities? The police?"

"No," Leeland jumped in—*ready*, Laoch thought, *with another smooth lie.* "Our father was calling to us as he was taken away into the sky . . . he kept saying the same thing over and over—"

"And what was he saying, Leeland?" Mr. Moongate asked gently.

Sty and Nudge eyed each other uneasily.

"Run, boys, run. Run away from here and go north!"

"That's understandable," Mr. Moongate responded, though again Laoch felt as if he was thinking something else altogether. "Well, I'm *very* sorry to hear about your parents, and I hope they are returned safe and sound very soon. I wish I could help in that department, but I'm just a Western Winged Postman, you see—" and he pointed at a small insignia on the lapel of his blue uniform.

"Yes of course," Laoch replied. "We're just glad to have met up with you."

"Me too, my boy, me too. And it seems we're all headed in the same direction now . . . I'm going up to make a pass through Utomia, and then to the plains north of there, so I can set you on your way for a bit. How does that sound?"

"Good!" all four youngsters replied at once. Nudge giggled nervously, not quite sure what to think about the half-truths the brothers had been telling. Laoch, meanwhile, couldn't believe their luck. If Mr. Moongate was heading to Utomia, that meant he could guide them the entire way. *Who needs a map now?!* he thought.

"Very well, then," the postman continued, hefting his bag a few inches higher on his shoulder. "I suppose we'd better get going. Follow me. And be quick about it. We don't want to be detected—it is still quite dangerous."

A few hours passed as the boys followed Mr. Moongate into the darkness of the plains. Laoch trailed him effortlessly, not minding the path he picked, for there was no visible course. Just acres and acres of softly blowing grass. This was a new sensation, for all the pathways in Talamh were tried and true, and ingrained in his mind like a fingerprint.

The sound of their footfalls through the lush reeds was rhythmic and calming. Still, Laoch knew that somewhere in that darkness, not so very far behind them, a billowy column of purple smoke continued to extend to the high heavens. And he, Laoch, was responsible for it.

He tried to picture his parents. They were being transported to Creight, Sty had said. What did this look like? Were they in a wagon, or on the backs of Bison? Were they passed off to the Other Bats, or put in cages? Or worse: carried in the sharp talons of Dragons—

He tried to focus on the stars overhead in an effort to blot out these images. But it was no use. What had his father meant? His *path*? The disc? *BORN. LIVE. DIE*, he recalled, another confounding phrase he'd heard his father use countless times. What did it even mean? What did anything mean when one's parents had been kidnapped? When they could be hurt, or worse—

A sickness rose in his stomach as he choked back a violent sob. He did not want the others to hear. *I must stay strong for them*, he thought. Especially Leeland. Even though they were twins, he had always seemed the older of the two, and always looked out for him. He realized now that he'd always felt this was, somehow, his duty.

"*BORN. LIVE. DIE,*" he repeated under his breath. The hated mantra that *never* made any sense—for it seemed too vague to mean anything at all.

But now a different notion washed over him.

Laoch repeated the phrase in his mind. *You are BORN . . . this you do not choose. You DIE . . . this you also do not choose. But to LIVE . . .*

To Live. To be on a path that cannot be followed, only chosen. To take responsibility for one's own self, one's own destiny. Could that be it?

But what *was* his destiny? He had just failed at his biggest experiment—would he become an inventor yet? And now, with his parents gone, perhaps his destiny was to be a no-madic orphan, displaced and wandering the land forever. *But if I CHOOSE a different way . . .* he began to think, *then will I truly be living? How do I know if my choices are leading me toward my destiny or not?*

He wished his father were there so he could ask him these pressing questions. The meaning behind the cryptic mantra glimmered in and out of focus as he walked on through the night. Uneasiness crept over him again. For practically his entire life it had been his dream to leave Talamh. But now the feeling of the open terrain surrounding him was alarming. Every few minutes he jerked his head to confront the unseen dangers he was sure were lurking all around. But there was only the face of his brother behind him. Or more eerily, nothing at all.

After an hour or so of this solemn parade, Mr. Moongate, a jolly sort of fellow, despite the circumstances, began to entertain the boys with stories of his travels. The rest of the nighttime hours passed easily, and for the time being Laoch was distracted from the thoughts heavy on his mind.

None of the boys had previously spent much time thinking about Mr. Moongate, nor that he might be anyone special. Now they realized that this was an oversight. For as a traveling postman, he had seen more places—and had more interesting experiences—than practically anyone else they'd ever met. In the Northeastern Woodlands, he had stayed with Illuminated Frogs, who live their lives entirely off the ground; had gazed upon phosphorescence that emerges only on the full moon in the farthest edge of the Cascade Sea, and joined the strange horned water creatures that bathe in its light. He'd traveled to the north of Utomia with bands of trickster gypsy Meerkats known for stealing travelers' shoes, and conversed with talking spiders of the Iron Mountains, relating to the boys the strange lies they spun (for they cannot tell the truth).

The youngsters listened in awe until finally Mr. Moongate halted and declared it time to set up camp for the night. Not knowing what this meant exactly, they watched as he expertly unrolled one of his packs and spread out a sleeping blanket, then balled up an extra jacket for a pillow. He asked Nudge and Leeland to gather the woody stems of plainsbrush for a fire (which they did tentatively, not wanting to stray too far from the others in the darkness). Sty—though sleepy, for he did not get his daytime nap—caught two rabbits, and before Laoch knew it Mr. Moongate had started a small but very warm fire. The five of them huddled around its warmth until finally the postman suggested they turn in for the night. They'd be rising early "to get a good start on the day" as he put it.

With that, all four boys crawled under their blankets and lay quietly, the sound of the fire crackling by their sides. They did not speak as one by one they fell asleep.

There were no words for what had happened that day.

Laoch nodded off like the others, but his sleep was restless, and a few hours later he woke with a start. He bolted upright, still surrounded by darkness. The fire had all but burned out and only a few red coals remained.

He scanned the shapes arranged around him. Mr. Moongate. Leeland. Nudge. Sty . . .

Sty?

His blanket lay flat on the ground.

Ah well, I'm sure he's out keeping watch, Laoch thought, reminding himself that his friend was built for the night hours. Still, a chill set over his body and he cinched the blanket up around his neck. He thought for a moment that he might wake Mr. Moongate just in case something was amiss, but before he could stir his breathing became quiet and even, and he drifted off to sleep.

Chapter 18
THE CALL OF THE OTHERS

eeland was the first to open his eyes the next morning. His back ached from lying on the hard ground and the end of his nose was cold. He'd been dreaming. And while it was no extraordinary dream—he'd been in the shop with the Master Cobbler, working silently (on shoes, of course)—it left him feeling calm and content. How he loved that shop! How he loved his tools. The shaping of the leather. The small details of stitching.

A lump formed in his throat.

Those days, it seemed, were gone. At least for now.

Stretching, Leeland sat up and surveyed the scene. The morning sun tinged the tips of the grasses around them with peach and golden hues, and as far as the eye could see in any direction there was . . . nothing.

He glanced over at the others, their blankets still pulled over their heads.

That's when he noticed that something was not right.

He sprang to his feet, his head pounding a bit.

"Laoch!" he shouted, leaning over one of the lumpy shapes beside him. "Laoch, wake up!"

The lump groaned.

"Nudge! Sty! Get up!"

He strode over to the others and poked them with his feet.

"Cut it out," Nudge grumbled, turning over.

The sun rose higher in the sky, inch by inch, illuminating what was becoming—in Leeland's eyes—a glaring problem.

"I'm serious, wake *up*!"

Laoch rolled over and cast his blanket aside, muttering under his breath. He stood warily, stretching his arms, and watched his brother nervously pacing about.

That's when he saw it.

Mr. Moongate was missing.

"Oh *no no no no no*—" Laoch breathed, looking around in every direction. But it was true: there was absolutely *nothing* except miles and miles of plains, save one plot of forest in the far distance. And *no* sign of the postman.

"Wake up, you two," he said seriously, standing over Nudge and Sty, who reluctantly blinked their eyes into the morning sun.

"He's gone!" Leeland gushed. He didn't even have to say whom, for it was obvious to everyone that they were suddenly a party of four, not five.

"Where do you think he went?" Nudge asked, squinting at the vista.

"Maybe he forgot that he had an appointment—" Leeland replied, not wanting to think ill of Mr. Moongate, nor that he had abandoned them, for they had had such a pleasant time together overall.

Laoch laughed caustically.

"A meeting out *here*?" he said. "Are you kidding me? What kind of meeting is so important that he couldn't even say goodbye?" He shook his head angrily. He couldn't think of one good reason why the old postman would desert them out there with no idea which way to go, and no experience outside of Talamh whatsoever.

"Maybe he evaporated," Nudge giggled. Leeland and Sty cracked begrudging smiles. "Maybe he was just a ghost!"

More giggles ensued, and Nudge—who must have been *extremely* nervous about Mr. Moongate's disappearance—doubled over in what was a rather severe fit of laughter, even for him. However, no one else found the situation to be very funny.

"Argh!" Laoch shouted. "I can't take any more of your *ghost talk* right now!" He turned to Sty, who had yet to say a word.

"Sty, did *you* see where he went? You were keeping watch, right?"

"No, I didn't see anything—" Sty replied, looking down. One of his feet clawed the dirt.

"*Really*? Nothing at all? Weren't you flying above us? And why were you asleep this morning?" As Laoch spoke he realized that it was indeed quite unusual for his friend to rest at that time of day.

"I *was* keeping watch," Sty expounded slowly, "but I got tired . . . so I came down for a quick nap. He could have left when I was sleeping. Or . . . when I saw the rabbit hole."

Laoch shook his head. "The rabbit hole?"

"Yeah . . . It must have been really late. I saw some movement a couple hundred feet away . . . so I flew over to investigate, to make sure it wasn't anything dangerous. And there was this . . . hole in the ground. And at first I thought it was a Meerkat dwelling—"

"Hey!" Nudge exclaimed. Of course he knew that Meerkats had, for thousands of years, lived underground. But that was not the way of things in the Southern Hills, where all Beings lived in houses. It was seen as uncouth in some respects, to be a plains or desert Meerkat and to live in tunnels within the soil.

"Nudge, you *know* that's where they live out here—"

"Okay okay, I know, it's just weird—"

"Anyway," Sty continued, "I waited around the hole for awhile, and then—"

"And *then*?" Leeland asked (for he was certain the story would end with another atrocity, and he couldn't bear the suspense).

Sty shrugged, midair. "Then nothing." He paused and looked at the ground. "A little rabbit poked his face out, then went back inside."

Laoch looked away, exasperated at the boring explanation—though he and the others were secretly glad nothing more sinister had transpired. Still, that didn't solve their problem. "And then you came down for a *nap*?" he pressed. "Was Mr. Moongate here *then*?"

"I . . . I'm not sure—"

Laoch scowled, but Leeland patted Sty's head reassuringly.

"Don't worry, it's not your fault," he said quietly. "Of course you would have woken everyone up if you noticed he was gone."

Sty managed a small smile, and for a moment let his friend continue to comfort him. But then he pulled away and took to the air.

"I'm going to catch some breakfast," he called, and winged away from the others, hoping his explanation had satisfied them.

For there had been no rabbit hole in the night. And though it was true that he hadn't, in fact, seen Mr. Moongate steal away, it was not because he was investigating possible dangers, or sleeping.

He had flown back.

Their calls had been faint at first. Sty tried to ignore them, even, watching the fire and flying circles around their camp.

But after an hour of listening to the distant noises, it was no use. The strange buzzing inside him had returned, and before he knew it Sty had taken to the air (once the others nodded off, of course), pointed his wings in the direction from whence they came, and sailed silently through the dark sky back to Talamh.

It had not taken him long, for traveling by air was much quicker than by land, and within the hour he could see the small lights of the town twinkling in the distance below. His eyes, adjusted to the darkness, could also make out the deeper shadow of the smoke plume rising from the schoolhouse.

He flew a bit closer, but not so close as to pass over the village. Rather, he stayed on the outskirts and just listened, or rather *felt* the language of the Other Bats reverberate in his body.

"He is here," Sty heard, not knowing who *he* was.

"Where?" the Others cried, and another voice answered: "Invisible."

This silenced them for a moment.

"Has he crushed them?"

"Look at them run! Fools—"

"You can't hide from him!"

"Trying to save their children—"

"Where? Bring them here, I'm hungry for blood—"

"The baby Meerkats are the tastiest!"

"How they squeal! How they squeal!"

The Other Bats' cries rose into a frenzied pitch, and Sty's stomach lurched. "NO!" his heart screamed, yet he remained silent lest they hear him, detect his presence, come for him, devour him . . .

He started to shiver so violently that it became difficult to fly. His body began to lose elevation.

The calls continued. Different now. Questions.

"Who started the smoke?"

"What do you mean you don't know? Do you want to die?!"

It became obvious then that the Other Bats were interrogating the townspeople. Their frightened responses Sty could only imagine, for that kind of language could not travel so far. His body quivered and rolled. He was falling, and fast.

His eyes widened as the ground came closer—this had never happened to him before.

The image of his friends flashed through his mind, and he saw them in their tree house. Saw Nudge's face when he was overcome with laughter; Laoch pointing up at the tree, directing them in their progress; Leeland's brow furrowed with concentration as he painted yet another camouflaged shingle. Then he imagined all three of them: sweetly, innocently asleep in the plains behind him with no one watching over them, no protection against . . .

At the last moment, shuddering and falling and mere feet from the ground, Sty pulled it together. He stretched out his wings, forcing a small grunt, and just like that the shuddering stopped and he swooped gracefully in a wide U above the ground and then *up up up*, heading back to the plains as fast as he could with a strong resolve in his heart.

As he flew to the campsite—his eyes tearing from the rush of the cool night air and the thought of abandoning his friends, even for an hour or two—Sty realized that he was not alone, and that he only had one family, and they were it, and no Bats could ever change that.

When he'd returned, however, and landed among them, checking frantically to make sure they were all there, breathing and safe, he had seen it.

The spot where Mr. Moongate had lain down for the night was missing something.

He'd flown up. Scanned in every direction. Listened for any sign of movement.

But . . . there was nothing.

So little Sty, exhausted from both the flight and the guilt welling within—*I should have been keeping watch!* he thought. *What will I tell everyone when they see he's missing?*—finally flew down to ground level and crawled under his own blanket, willing himself to sleep.

"Those weren't very big," Nudge lamented, his stomach still growling. He squatted, poking a stick into the fire they'd revived. Sty had returned with two small rabbits and the boys had cooked and eaten them ravenously while deciding what to do next.

Laoch was having the same thought. His stomach grumbled as he rolled up his blanket, carefully reassembling his pack.

Leeland—who had neatly packed his things hours ago, being that sort of fellow—was gazing out toward the stand of forest dotting the infinite grass, perhaps a mile or two away from their campsite. It was as if someone had just plunked it there, much like the Smelderlings in the wheat fields outside of Talamh.

"I wonder why we didn't stop *there* for the night," he mused.

Both Laoch and Nudge looked up, shading their eyes from the early morning rays. Mystified, they said nothing. Nor did Sty, who was quietly waiting for the others to finish packing so they could be on their way. Quietly trying not to look quite so guilty. Quietly trying to forget all the madness he had heard. Quietly trying to forget the sensation that had come over him when he felt their awful voices . . .

"Seriously, though," Laoch said abruptly, turning to face the little Bat. "You can see so far out here, and for so long, that even if you went to scare up a rabbit I think you would have spotted Mr. Moongate leaving at *some* point."

The others were now staring at him too.

"I just don't get how you missed it."

They were not buying his story.

"I *told* you already," he replied, darting about in the air. "I *was* keeping watch, but then I left to investigate the rabbit hole. When I got back, I didn't notice anything strange, so I came down for a nap. He must have left when I was asleep."

Laoch shook his head, still perplexed by the matter.

"Well, did you see *anything* else? While you were awake, I mean."

"No, not really," the Bat replied. He landed a few feet away and stared down at the dirt (for he could not bear to look his friends in the eyes). "I saw another rabbit or two, but that was it. It was pretty boring, to tell you the truth."

"Speaking of your sleep patterns," Leeland interjected, "how are you going to rest if we're on the move in the daytime?"

All four boys looked at one another. This was something they hadn't considered—including Sty—and just the thought of spending another whole day awake made him yawn.

Always good in these situations, Nudge quickly untied the red bandanna from around his neck (that the others often teased him about, to which he would reply, rather honestly: "It's just so my parents can tell me apart from my brothers!"), and quickly fashioned a carrying sack of sorts, which rested on his back.

"See, Laoch?" he exclaimed. "You're not the only one who can invent things!" He spun around to show off his handiwork. "Sty, when you get tired you can crawl in here and I'll carry you!"

"You can't carry him the whole way—" Laoch began, thinking it would probably slow them down, and perhaps it wasn't such a good idea for Sty to come along after all.

"Sure I can," Nudge insisted. "I need the extra training anyhow. Remember, I'm not going to some stupid old city with you guys, I'm going to the—"

"*Water Games*, yes, we *know*," Laoch finished, watching Sty squeeze into the sling. Nudge leapt and pounced around them to prove the worthiness of the arrangement—and to be true, Sty remained snug against his back. So Laoch just shrugged and finished packing his things.

Soon enough they were ready to set out, but no one knew which way to go.

"Which way do you think is north?" Leeland asked.

"That way," Sty said, reaching his wing out of the sack and pointing.

"How do you know?"

"I just . . . do," he replied sleepily. The rhythmic jostle of Nudge's gate was having an effect on him not unlike a baby being rocked by its mother.

"*I just do* is not going to cut it," Laoch interjected.

"Oh I don't know, Laoch, I believe Sty—" Leeland argued. For it made perfect sense that the only one of them who could fly would be able to get their bearings much easier than those bound by the land. This he patiently explained to his brother.

Laoch prodded the Bat in the hope of verifying the theory, but received only a tired moan in response.

"Well I agree with Leeland," Nudge concluded. He struck off in the direction Sty had signaled, and Leeland followed. But after only a few steps, it became apparent that Laoch was not coming with. Rather, it appeared that he had picked up a piece of dead grass and was holding it in the wind.

"C'mon, Laoch! What are you doing?"

"I'm trying to figure out if this is the right plant," he muttered.

"What?" his brother called. *"I can't hear you!"*

"I'll be right there!" Laoch yelled back, then continued under his breath: "Three twining leaves every handswidth." He measured the stalk against his fingers. "Resistance to breaking." He tugged on either end of the specimen and nodded. "Aerial roots." He reached into his pocket and pulled out a small magnifier, one of the most oft-used tools back in his laboratory. Squinting, he held it to his face, and lo and behold, there they were: tiny, almost-invisible root structures hanging off the stem.

Traveler's vine, he thought excitedly. He'd never seen it before. Not with his own eyes. He sank to his knees and scanned the ground, pushing aside the tall grasses to reveal even *more* vines forming an abundant undergrowth. And sure enough, they all ran in one direction.

When he caught up to the others, Laoch skipped with confidence to the front of the posse. "Sty was right, it's this way," he told them, gesturing ahead. "I verified it by the Traveler's Vine. It only grows on meridians from north to south."

"Oh yeah? Where'd you learn that trick?" Nudge teased. "Romantic after-school sessions with Whakdak?"

Laoch cracked a smile and socked him in the side.

"Ouch!" Sty squeaked, then promptly fell still again.

"Never you mind where I learned it," Laoch answered. "What we need to do is keep that spot of forest"—he pointed to the distant stand of trees Leeland had noticed earlier—"on our left. That'll keep us on track, even where the vine isn't growing."

What neither Laoch nor the others knew, however, was that indeed he had *not* found the fabled Traveler's Vine. Nevertheless, he boldly continued on. "Utomia has *got* to be just over the next couple of knolls . . . *I can feel it.*"

"*I can feel it* is not going to cut it," Leeland mimicked under his breath. Because they were twins, it was easy for him to see when Laoch cared more about being right—or at least *seeming* right—then about what was *actually* true. For Leeland had his doubts about how long it would take them to reach the city. *If Talamh is truly this close to Utomia,* he mused, *wouldn't Beings tend to travel there more often? Even just to take a look?*

But he kept these thoughts to himself, and given their circumstances, tried his best to remain hopeful.

"UTOMIA HERE WE COME!" Laoch shouted to the sky, throwing excited fists into space as they began the day's trek.

"UTOMIA HERE WE COME!" Nudge echoed, leaping and bounding ahead. Even Leeland, letting go of his trepidation, let out a short *whoop* in support of their adventure, and the three of them, for a time, howled joyfully into the great nothingness, the little Bat not stirring a bit.

But beneath all of Laoch's wild calls, he felt nervous about the day ahead. The creepy feeling the plains had given him the night before hadn't gone away in the daylight. They were exposed on all sides. And the pocket of forest—an anomaly against the straight horizon—loomed in the distance, a dark beacon on the endless swath of wavy green.

Chapter 19
THE HEART OF THE MATTER

"We are the eyes, we are the ears. I know, I know. I *know* this. But what about the heart? Is it so impossible? Impossible to be the heart?"

[…]

"And yet how can we go on without it?"

His own heart beat heavily beneath a tattered overcoat. He stood pristine against the waving grasses that reached almost to his waist, arms extended wide toward the endless vista as if he were a falcon riding thermals to the sun. And yet. He darted his eyes. He lowered his voice. A warm breeze unfurled over the waving stalks and caught the wiry fluff of his arm.

"What about my fur? Of course I mean this rhetorically."

[. . .]

"It's gray. Gray as stone. Such is the price of this vocation."

[. . .]

"While my love lingers on, I will be long dead and gone."

[. . .]

"Aaaargh."

[. . .]

"But we need *one of us* to see things with our own eyes, no?"

[. . .]

"To *speak* with them face-to-face."

[. . .]

"'Tis no use—"

The incessant cry of crickets rose to a mournful din. His ears twitched. Without moving a muscle, his eyes flitted over the horizon before blinking, hard. He'd slept little these past days.

"I'm sorry—I become sentimental when war is afoot."

Across the expanse, a distinct purple column rose into the sky.

"You have no idea the perils of this land. But I see them. To the south, 'twas more horror than expected."

[. . .]

"It is happening as we knew it would—"

[. . .]

"A'flight. Two of them, and their master. I saw a Being . . . crushed. Her mind grew—"

[. . .]

"Moldy."

For a moment he held his breath, then shivered. A windswept rush of meadow blossomed toward him like ripples on a lake.

"Four of them. Utterly alone. And soon to be more so, if I may wager how this will unfold—"

[. . .]

"Taken. And doubtful to return."

[. . .]

"Could not stay with them for long, naturally."

[. . .]

"To interfere would be—"

[. . .]

"Their own journey to make. And a painful one at that."

[. . .]

"They do not understand what *is*. Nor what is coming."

He cleared his throat. And yet nothing changed. The grasses continued their gentle sway.

"No map."

[. . .]

"No sense of direction."

[. . .]

"Of course the most adventurous are always the most foolhardy."

[. . .]

"Now if you mention my youthful follies, I'll tie your arms in a knot!"

[. . .]

"Great danger. The tide is turning."

[. . .]

"I'm off, for there are many miles to go. *Magespeed.*"

[. . .]

With that, the postman shook his outstretched arms up and down, just once. The six songbirds who perched there, quiet but listening, simply fell into the air and began to sail toward the clouds.

"Magespeed," he whispered to the wind that carried them.

Then the scruffy old Meerkat was alone once again. The plains extended forlornly until they swept the sky, marred by nothing but a strange purple cloud to the south.

Thinking of the likely fate of his old friend, his stomach sank.

Thinking of his friend's sons, and their companions, his heart hurt.

For he knew better than anyone that the road ahead was always long, and never what one expected.

So, with much heaviness in his stride, the postman patted his bundle of parcels and set off in silence.

Meanwhile, the six songbirds rose quickly in a vertical line. About a mile off the ground they veered from one another in coordinated dispersal, much how berries of wheat bend off the stalk.

One bird flew south—south to the place where the purple smoke rose and Bats clouded the sky like ash. Where somewhere in a viney wood a tree house sat in silence.

Another winged northwest until a blue jewel appeared in the distance, shimmering between the plains and the sky. When it reached the sea, the bird dropped to water level and raced over the waves. Shapes appeared below. One-two-three they came, four-limbed and silent under translucent water, when *POP!*—the shapes emerged, gasping for air, arms swinging with perfect grace. As the Meerkats swam for the finish line and calls of the crowd crescendoed into din, the bird swung high above them all and landed within a small city perched upon the shore.

Another bird pushed farther north—more northerly than most ventured to fly. Great mountains jutted into the sky. The bird rested here and there on craggy ledges (for the air was thin and dry and very cold), before surging onward.

A fourth made its way north and east, crossing long stretches of monotonous plains until forests emerged that stretched far as the eye could see, giving the impression of forever. Tendrils of smoke rose from the dense canopy, fragrant with sacred herbs. The rhythmic calls of Tree Frogs permeated the rush of wind, and the bird sang as it flew, old melodies marking the passage of distance and time.

The fifth bird sailed west. It watched as grassland turned to red clay dappled with dust storms in the distance. Nomadic travelers moved like insects upon the sand. The bird watched mirages appear and disappear, and black smoke lifted off lava fields into the ever-darkening skies.

The sixth and final bird flew ahead of the postman. It winged north over the small towns not a day's walk from the great city. The immense grasslands beyond were dizzying in their monotony, though the bird sped straight as an arrow. It did not twist along the arteries of surface undulations—dried-up riverbeds unseen from the ground but stark from above, imprinting the land with the stamp of barren networks. It continued until a half sphere, like a partially buried fish egg, appeared in the distance. The shape grew and grew in size until it became wider and higher than anything else around; until it became humungous. The songbird circled above until it spied a green flag waving near one of the Portals—a sure sign there was a Bird Box nearby.

It dove toward the opening, past the two Guards keeping watch, and presently spotted a square protrusion jutting from the Outer Wall. It landed inside the box, and was swiftly processed through the Shield before sailing *up up up* and out of the Between, over the Inner Wall, and into the thick city air, humming with activity.

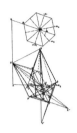

Chapter 20

THE OLDEST OF THEM ALL

Rap-a-tap-tap-tap! went the window.

Dosha startled and lifted his head from his task. He squatted near the kitchen counter (this being his most oft-assumed position, as he extolled the many benefits of frequent snacks on one's intellect and ingenuity), while his automatic dusting apparatus misfired in his arms.

"Come in!" he called to the bird hovering just outside the glass.

The end of the gizmo's arm, which was a rather diminutive but effective broom made of fine silk-straw (another one of his inventions), yanked itself out of his grasp and slapped him clear across the face with a loud *SMACK!*

"Oh BLAST! Come IN!" he yelled again with more force, and tossed the backfiring doodad to the ground.

The bird, who rather disliked being indoors, flew warily over the accouterments of the sprawling abode.

"Don't land on the tubing!" Dosha instructed. The bird continued to circle, unsure where to go. Meanwhile, the dusting contraption continued to gyrate and thud on the floor as the coo-coo clock began to chime. At *this* point, the arm for making tea was set into motion and shot down the length of the room on its track, nearly swatting the poor bird as it darted about.

"Must I always hold the hand of those around me?" the inventor muttered. "Very well. If I *must*, I *must*."

Turning to face the bird (as best he could, for again it was flitting about in the most maddening of ways), he more commanded than requested that it so *kindly* meet him in the study.

With that, and only two hops across the room, the corpulent Toad landed back in his favorite chair. He dug a modest skill crystal out of his knickerbockers and placed it in a metal cup at the base of the lamp beside him. A soft light emanated over the room, and shortly thereafter the songbird perched atop the lampshade, the tea was poured and brought to him (by the tea-delivering arm), and for the moment all was set right again. They sat together like that for a spell, until eventually the old inventor nodded and cleared his throat.

"But they aren't even orphans yet!" he exclaimed. "They're only *potential* orphans."

The bird stared at him blankly.

"Have YOU a mother or father?"

(It was certainly not customary to speak of personal matters with a bird.)

(Though Dosha rarely minded customs.)

But again, the bird said nothing.

So, with a deep sigh, Dosha flicked four fingers toward the window. The feathered visitor immediately took flight, circled once more over the lab table, and exited the apartment much in the same manner it had appeared.

Dosha remained in his chair, contemplating the visit.

"It's not *so* bad to be on one's own—"

He looked around as if someone might answer him, but of course no one did. The clock ticked. The broken contraption thumped pathetically at the other end of the apartment.

"And what in the crystal crossfire"—a common Utomian expression, of course—"is so *terrible* about being an orphan anyway?"

Dosha peered up at the ceiling. Etched in the plaster was a painting he had commissioned long ago. It was aged now. Darkened with soot. Covered in dust and cobwebs. Rare was it for Beings who visited his abode to notice the artwork, but to him it was ever-present. For it depicted his parents, both venerable Beings in their own right—or so he'd been told—at their humble home in the Southern Hills.

For it was true what they said about him in the old days. He was not Utomian-born. But those who knew this eventually passed on, and today no Being was the wiser.

Except for Dosha himself, of course. For he was the oldest of them all.

Reclining even farther into his chair, the Toad studied the portrait with great solemnity. He had no real memories of his parents, but he'd described to the artist in great detail how he envisioned them in his mind's eye. Each with a gentle smile. Flowers in the garden. A quaint walkway to the house. *A happy place*, he thought warmly.

No, even as the world forgot his true origins, he would never let slip from his memory that he'd come to this existence on the Outside—much like his departed apprentice Frederick.

"Although he was worth but a whistle," the old Toad mused. "Nevertheless," he continued. "There may be others. One never does know."

With that, he heaved his portly frame from the chair and made his way back to the kitchen, where with great effort (for his flexibility had lagged considerably over the last hundred years) he bent over the flip-flopping dusting appliance.

"Now, where *were* we?"

As he fiddled with the broken arm, it began to hit him once again—this time in the throat. The silk-straw, oh so very soft, tickled him mightily and despite himself, with every smack, Dosha released a giggle that sounded like:

Ribbit! Ribbit!

Rather uncomfortable with the arrangement, the wise old Toad steadied his gaze.

Ribbit!

He sized up the track and marked the angle.

Ribbit!

He yanked down on the upper phalange and rotated the arm in a wide circle.

Ribbit! Ribbit! Ribbit!

Then, before it could slap his throat even once more, the arm hooked into place and much like his tea-pouring arm, and his tea-*delivering* arm, set off down the track and began to furiously dust the bookshelves in his study. This in turn kicked quite a lot of detritus into the air, and just as Dosha began to cough, the coo-coo clock chimed once again, signaling dinnertime.

Feeling that his work for the day was quite done, the lone inventor hopped his way to the boudoir section of the apartment where he donned his best houndstooth vest (in fact his *only* houndstooth vest), his cane, and a handsome green-and-brown beret.

"I dare say, this has been a productive day," he commented happily as he hopped out the front door. "A *very* productive day indeed."

Once outside, however, Dosha's smile disappeared. He could still see the plume of purple smoke in the distant sky, waving through the Water Shield.

"Magespeed," he whispered to no one in particular, then followed the stone pathway between his home and his neighbor's, where he was destined to share a fine, plentiful meal with exceptional company in a home much like the one he never had.

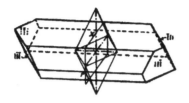

Chapter 21

AN INVISIBLE CLOAK

O n the fourth day, the boys staggered on.

They had traveled at a good clip, but not much seemed to change along the way. There was no sign of Utomia, nor any other town for that matter. No sign of Mr. Moongate. And no sign of water, their supply running dangerously low.

The boys' conversation too became as monotonous as the fields around them. Every few hours they wondered aloud how long it would take them to reach Utomia or the Cascade Sea—and for that matter, in what order they should visit them. This question led them to realize that they had no idea which they'd encounter first, or when, so it was decided that they'd just have to take it as it came, for some things could not be planned.

Still, the unknown was having an effect on their spirits.

"Remind me why we decided to come out here without a map?" Nudge asked. He adjusted his pack, which hung over his front side, as well as the sling for Sty, which was worn on his back, and whose straps dug terribly into his shoulders.

"Some of us apparently aren't tough enough for this kind of thing," Laoch shot back. He meant it in jest, but no one smiled. Though they rarely bickered back at the tree house, patience was another resource that was becoming increasingly scarce.

I'm tough, Leeland thought. *But that doesn't mean I want to die out here.* He looked down at his feet. They were covered in sores inside his shoes—shoes he had of course made himself. But the craftsmanship wasn't the problem. Rather, there was precious little water left (and in fact he'd had nothing to drink in over a day in the hope of saving his last reserves for when he needed them most). Because of this, his scales—normally dewy and bright—were cracked and dull. His feet split under the constant stress of movement without rest, and his face and arms blistered under a sun without shade.

The others were in not much better condition.

"I'm *so thirsty,*" Nudge complained. He stopped walking and fell to his knees on the hot ground.

"Get up," Laoch urged, trying to lift him by the shoulders. But Nudge wouldn't move.

"Get up!" he said more strongly.

Again, nothing.

"I don't think I can."

Nudge coughed. His throat was dry as dust. It was true that he had run out of water before the others, but no one seemed to remember that he was carrying a whole other Being on his back. For hours and hours a day. Every day.

"You have to," Laoch commanded, heaving his friend's shoulders a third time. This caused Nudge to flop forward onto all fours. Sty was roused from the commotion and took to the air, looking a bit befuddled.

"What's going on?" he squeaked.

"Nudge has decided not to go on," Laoch replied bitterly. Oh and he *was* bitter. For he had watched the Meerkat guzzle his water intemperately ever since they embarked upon their journey. Why, he was gulping it down even as they were leaving Talamh. And despite warnings from everyone, he'd not modified his behavior one bit. Which of course meant he'd run clean out of water two days ago. *It's no one's fault but his own*, Laoch thought. *He has no right to hold us back just because he can't control himself.*

"You can have my water."

Leeland bent over his friend, offering his canteen.

The others, including Nudge, looked at him in disbelief.

"Really?" both Nudge and Laoch replied in unison.

"Take it. *Drink*," Leeland insisted. Then he pressed the last of his reserves into his friend's paws. Nudge said nothing, but bowed his head. There were no words for such kindnesses. Then he drank heartily, every last drop.

Soon Nudge was back on his feet and the foursome moved along once again. The others chatted amiably to pass the time, but Laoch was silent. *What a foolish thing to do!* he fumed. But then another voice popped into his head—one he'd been trying to suppress for the last few days.

A black cloak, invisible to the others, hung from his shoulders. He knew it was there, and yet he tried fiercely to ignore it. Still. He sensed it. Heavy on his arms. Pinching at his neck. Hot like fire upon his back. Catching between his legs and under his feet—

The cloak weighed him down. It whispered into his ears:

Why aren't you the kind of Being who would offer your water to your best friend when he is suffering?

He tugged at his collar.

What did you think would become of you out here?

He adjusted his belt.

What did you think would become of your parents?

He wiggled his jaw and cracked his knuckles.

Who is responsible for all of this?!

Without warning, Laoch threw off his pack and jerked furiously at his shirt, popping off a button as he yanked it over his head.

The others watched with wide-eyed concern.

"You don't look so good, pal," Nudge said, poking him in the arm. "Are you okay?"

"You do seem a bit pale—" Sty added, winging overhead.

Leeland bent down to pick up his brother's pack. "We can stop for a bit if you like," he said gently, handing it back to him. "I think we could all use the rest."

The others nodded, but Laoch refused.

"I'm *fine*," he insisted, brushing them off. "I was just hot." The others eyed him dubiously, so he stretched his bare arms out in either direction. "Plus, I figured that since the scenery is a little drab out here, you might like a gander at *these* fine specimens." He flexed his arm and chest muscles in a few different poses, and the other boys cracked up.

Though Laoch laughed along with them, the seriousness of their situation was never far from his thoughts. He scanned the landscape, racking his mind for more ways to find water. He'd already tried dowsing, and sucking on Water Grass. He even dug a hole. Nothing seemed to work.

"We can't afford to take breaks anymore," he added gravely. "Not with two of us out of water. We've got to keep moving if we're ever going to—"

He didn't finish his sentence, but he didn't have to.

As they trekked on, Leeland—to distract himself from these troubling realities, as well as the burning blisters on his feet—tried to think of more pleasant things. Namely, cobbling. He tried to re-create his workbench in his mind: which tools went where, and such. This was harder than he initially thought, for a good Cobbler has at least thirty-five or more instruments with which to work the leather, and Leeland (attempting to recall them all), counted at least forty-two.

The other boys kept their minds on similarly diverting matters. Nudge kicked the dirt every now and then, soundlessly mouthing chants to an imaginary crowd (now that he was not *quite* so parched). And while Sty flew drowsily above them, recalling the beauty of his fruit groves back in Talamh, Laoch kept his eyes on the horizon, anticipating the jewel of a city to rise up at any moment and call to him like a shining trumpet in the sky.

And so like this, for awhile longer, they kept on.

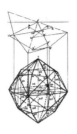

Chapter 22

AND THEN THE SKY
BEGAN TO FALL

I t was nearing noon on the fifth day when Laoch heard thunder faintly echo in the distance. *Not now, please not now,* he thought glumly. He didn't even want to consider what it would be like to spend a day—or worse, a night—in a thunderstorm out there. With no cover, they wouldn't be able to keep a fire going. And without a fire, it would surely get very, very cold. . . .

"Do you hear that?"

"What?" Nudge asked. "The sound of the crowds watching me win the Water Games?. . . *and he weaves left, ladies and gentlemen . . . and he weaves right . . . we've never seen a Being in the* land *cut through the water with such grace, such acumen . . . and he's coming through to the finish line . . . and he's won! Woooo! The crowd goes wild—"*

Nudge mock-swam in front of them, moving his arms in a circular fashion, and took a few quick steps before breaking down in a victory dance: pumping his arms, waving to a fake crowd, and continuing to howl with delight.

"Stop it Nudge, I'm serious. Pipe down!" Laoch admonished.

The boys walked on in silence. Then Leeland heard it too.

"Thunder, right?"

"Wait a second!" Laoch blurted suddenly. Why, if there was *thunder*, then that meant there would be *rain*, which meant—"Water!" he yelled. "If it rains, then we'll have WATER!"

Everyone looked up eagerly. Even Sty peeked his face out of the carrying sling, for Nudge's wild movements had roused him. "But the sky is clear," he mused.

"Except for the smoke," Leeland added. The others craned their necks to check, even though they knew in their hearts it was true: the purple smoke column was still visible behind them, even after all these days.

"Who cares about that now," Laoch insisted. He lifted his face to the sky. "Come on, thunder!" he yelled passionately. "LEMME HAVE IT!"

As the boys walked on, the low rumble grew louder and louder by the second. Sty crawled out of his sack and swung up to get a better view of the surrounding area.

"Do you *feel* it?" Leeland asked nervously, and Laoch was just about to say yes, yes he did, for the thunder seemed not to be coming from the air at all but from the ground itself, when there in the distance, over a far crest in the seemingly endless sea of grasses, came a mighty wall of figures, appearing quickly and moving straight toward them.

"Look!" Nudge cried, jumping up and down.

Sty squinted. He scanned the sky for Other Bats or Dragons but there were none—all of the Beings were land-bound. And just as they started to come into focus, he realized who they were.

"It's an army!" he squeaked from above. "Not the Other Army . . . the *Utomians!*"

"What?!" Laoch hollered up at him.

"What do we *DO*?" Leeland cried, and Nudge wrung his hands, both of them looking at Laoch until Nudge screamed *"Look!"* and pointed over Laoch's shoulder. They whipped around to see more swarms of Beings coming from the south, the direction of Talamh, most of them in the air but others on foot . . .

"RUN!" Laoch shouted, and took off to the west toward the dark swath of forest they'd been wondering about for the past few days. It seemed to be the only available cover in any direction. Nudge and Leeland followed, and Sty led the way by air, terrified as he was.

"Sty, you fly ahead! Don't wait for us!" Laoch yelled. "The Armies might mistake you for one of—"

Sty nodded, for he knew what Laoch meant. He zoomed ahead toward the woods, which seemed both impossibly far and impossibly near. The others followed as quickly as they could, the thunderous pounding of the land shaking their legs as they ran. And now they could hear other things—great clangs of metal and the shouts of terrifying Beings coming from everywhere at once.

Nudge looked wildly from side to side, yelling to his friends: "They're gaining on us! They're coming too fast!" Great shadows started to glide over the ground.

"Dragons!" Sty squealed, and Laoch glanced up, sure that one was headed straight for them, to pick them off like field mice. But it wasn't paying any attention to the boys at all. Rather, its body was surging through the air toward the Utomians, who were yelling war whoops and barking commands as they neared. Laoch's heart pounded as the beast sailed overhead.

"LOOK OUT!" he screamed as the Utomians shot a slew of long spears toward the Dragon, peppering the air. Then, fantastically, as if the sky was beginning to fall, the spears arched and dove, plunging deep into the earth around them at frightening angles. The boys thought at any moment they'd be hit, but somehow—through frantic dodging, but mostly just luck— they escaped the barrage.

The Dragon overhead was not so lucky. Laoch watched as one last spear pierced its side, sending it careening through the air and toppling with great speed to the ground. Before any of them could do much, it slammed against the dirt only a few yards away and all three were blown back. The ground rocked as the boys toppled over, their faces blasted with dust and debris.

"Get up! Keep going! The Armies aren't after us, they're after each other!" Laoch commanded, pulling his brother, who had tears streaming down his face to his feet. Sty had almost reached the trees ahead, and Laoch repeated over and over in his mind: *Just make it to the forest, just make it to the forest*, until miraculously, within a minute or two, it seemed closer and he could make out the details of lush undergrowth that gave way to taller, piney-looking woods beyond.

The boys were close to reaching the forest's edge when another screeching howl emerged from the sky. All three looked up in terror as another Dragon—this one even bigger than the first—hurdled down to the ground not twenty yards away. It hit with an everlasting thud, and the boys winced, sure to be smote at any moment. For this Dragon was not dead, and it reeled its head around, wildly scanning the ground. But Laoch, who cracked one eye open (hoping to see death coming and not face it blindly), watched the Dragon simply pick up a few scattered spears with its great talons, then take off into the air, not concerned with them at all.

"KEEP GOING!" he yelled, urging the others on.

As they ran the final steps toward the trees, more and more shadows appeared overhead. They were smaller, faster, and Laoch knew instantly the Other Bats had come forth. For their cries were deafening, and though he shouted at his brother and Nudge—"KEEP RUNNING! WE'RE ALMOST THERE!"—he couldn't even hear his own words as they issued from his mouth.

Laoch watched Sty disappear into the leaf cover in front of them and counted down in his head—*twenty, nineteen, eighteen . . .*—for they were so close and he needed something to focus on. To hope for. He glanced back over his shoulder to make sure that Leeland was right on his heels, when he saw his brother running with all his might, though not quickly enough. At the exact moment Laoch turned, in fact, a troop of fiercely muscled Lizards and pummeling Meerkats engulfed Leeland in a flurry of bodies and armor, just as a line of gigantic, howling Bison charged into them from the opposite direction.

Laoch lost sight of his brother, who was caught right in the middle of the fray.

"LEELAND!" he screamed, taking a few steps back toward the carnage. The Lizards—larger, stronger, and more ferocious than he ever could have imagined—were clad in shining golden armor and velvet green vestiges. Their shields and long swords were lifted, their faces steeled for victory or death. And the Meerkats, just as ferocious with fangs bared and numbers that seemed to multiply right there on the field, leapt as the Bison, tusks thrashing, pummeled into them. The Meerkats clung to their backs, plunging their swords deep into the beasts' necks, blood exploding all around.

Laoch watched as a Lizard on horseback reared and held his shield high. He called to his troops, and his muscled, tattooed arms gleamed deep emerald green in the sunlight. As he righted his steed, with one graceful swing he slashed the neck of an attacking Bat, sending it to a bloody skid on the ground.

"LEELAND!" Laoch yelled again, his heart beating madly. He was in awe of the Utomians—their bravery and skill—but terrified all the same, for his brother was caught somewhere in that terrible mess. Little Leeland. Gentle, kind Leeland. There was no way he could . . .

But then suddenly, as if by magic, Leeland came running at top speed from amid the riotous clash. Covered in dirt and blood, there he was, Laoch's twin, charging with all his might and looking strangely fierce. Laoch threw himself at his brother, hugging him in disbelief.

"Leeland! You made it!" he screamed. He grabbed his brother's hand and the two of them took off once again for the trees where Nudge and Sty were already hiding. Within moments, they reached the forest's edge and dove in headfirst. They crawled on their bellies until they were well underneath the brush before collapsing, utterly exhausted.

"Laoch! Leeland! Over here!" the others called. Leeland was the first to spot Nudge and Sty crouching a bit farther in, so he began to crawl in their direction.

"No! It's not safe!" Laoch shouted. He threw his body over his brother's and pinned him down.

"LET ME GO!" Leeland shrieked with unnamable terror, piercing Laoch's heart to the core. He loosened his grip. He hadn't meant to hurt him. He'd only meant to protect—

But Leeland wriggled away and thrashed ahead through the brushwood. Laoch trailed him cautiously.

"Leeland—" he called, but his brother continued on until he reached the others. They grasped him with great affection and relief, and when Laoch appeared all three wiped the dirt and blood off the little Lizard's face. Nudge and Sty slapped his back, talking all at once. "How did you get through it? What was it like? What did you see? I'm so glad you made it! I always knew you were the toughest one of all!" they exclaimed, when a loud crash sounded overhead and everyone dropped to the forest floor, covering their heads.

The scaly orange back of a Dragon slashed through the outer edges of the woods as if tree trunks were mere twigs, then thudded to the forest floor body first. Its tail whipped through the branches, breaking every one, and reached almost to where the boys huddled on the ground.

So they weren't quite safe after all.

"Follow me!" Laoch yelled, but as he turned to run into the forest, another Being blasted through the tree line above—this time a large gray Bat with hairy wings and horrible red eyes. It flew to the ground, almost catching Nudge on the shoulder had he not leapt out of the way. The boys were stunned, and as the Bat lay there, injured but not quite dead, it hissed at them and bared its fangs, struggling to pull itself off the forest floor. Without hesitation, Nudge, who was closest, grabbed a broken branch that had landed nearby and ran with all his strength at the Being. The jagged end of the stick plummeted deep into the Bat's chest and it squealed so loudly that Sty shrank back, a phantom pang searing through his own rib cage. The boys watched as the creature's red eyes dulled, and the tongue lolled out, until all of them knew, finally, it was dead.

Nudge, the most stunned of all at his courageous feat, stood there motionless, staring at the stick protruding from the Bat's chest, when another crash sounded from above. Without any words the boys took off at top speed into the woods, running (and flying) as quickly as they could, leaping over felled logs and under branches, until the sound of the battle slowly receded and eventually they could hear nothing save the peaceful sounds of the forest around them.

Chapter 23

SPIDER, SPIDER, WHERE-ARE-YOU?

When they finally stopped, everyone doubled over, gasping for breath. None of them had ever run so much, or so quickly, or for so long, in their lives. They collapsed onto the soft ground and rolled onto their backs. It was then that they first encountered the great vision above them.

While fleeing the battle, no one had paid much attention to the peculiarities of the forest. But now it was overwhelming.

Everything, it seemed, in this forest was huge.

The trees were at least five times as wide and tall as normal trees, as were the pine needles they lay upon—a foot long each and soft as corn silk. Towering trunks spread into a complex lattice of branches a few hundred feet above the ground. And running from treetop to treetop, just underneath their densely leaved canopies, were giant webs. White and wispy, they billowed gently as petite furry critters scampered to and fro.

There were no Spiders to be seen, however, which relieved Sty. For they were the only Beings in the world he was truly afraid of. Even more than the Bats of the Other Army . . . or Bison, or Dragons. He couldn't explain why, but they made his blood run cold. And if in the night he'd ever flown through a web by mistake, it sent him home immediately in a panic, his mother reassuring him that there were no Spiders crawling around on his back, and so forth.

"Check it out!" Laoch exclaimed suddenly.

The others craned their necks in all directions.

"That Ladybug!" another called.

It was the size of Leeland's head.

"Over here, come on!"

Sty sprang to the air. A boulder, perhaps fifty feet in height and almost perfectly round, loomed before him. It was covered in moss of the deepest green, swarming with juvenile butterflies that could only be seen from the air. Examining its immensity, Sty exhaled with wonder, and Leeland noted that against the magnitude of the rock his friend appeared teensy as a mosquito.

Nudge had also risen, his exhaustion replaced with awe. "Check this out!" he yelled as he bolted up a woody vine. Thicker than him, it was covered in delicate pink flowers and wrapped like a snake around the trunk of an enormous pine. Everything was covered in fine droplets of iridescent dew that glistened in sunbeams breaking through the canopy, creating a dappled shimmer and sparkle in the air. "We should build a tree house *here*!" he called, swinging high above their heads and giggling with joy.

"Yeah!" Leeland yelled back, trying to scale it as well (though he was not as good a climber as Nudge), when Sty called to all of them:

"I think I found a path!"

They looked over to where their little winged friend stood just beyond a giant clover patch, and sure enough a thin footpath appeared between two massive trunks.

Not having a plan at the moment, nor any idea where they were, the four struck off down the twisty trail. Sty took the lead, coasting only a few feet above the ground (to remain as far as possible from the huge webs looming overhead). The others ambled behind, not with any particular haste, for there were so many distracting sights in this strange wood.

"There's *got* to be water here," Leeland observed. For the place just *felt* watery. Every leaf was damp, the soil fragrant with must.

"That's what *I* was saying," his brother replied matter-of-factly.

"No you didn't!" Nudge blurted out. He gripped another vine overhanging the trail and catapulted forward.

Laoch marched on, his expression rather soured. "Maybe you were too busy swinging on vines to hear me—"

"Stop trying to take credit for all of Leeland's ideas!" he shot back. "He's the one who survived the Armies. We should be listening to *him* now, not *you*."

He was joking, of course, for Nudge put scarce thought into their pecking order (perhaps because he had little ambition to lead). But his words fell between the brothers like stone wedges, driving even more space between them.

"It doesn't matter who thinks what, as far as water is concerned." Sty was once more the voice of reason. "As long as we *find* some."

"That's right," Leeland echoed. "That's all that matters."

He patted his brother's shoulder in an effort to make amends. Even if the others didn't realize it, he knew *exactly* why Laoch was so testy. Ever since they were young, whenever his brother was *truly* worried about something, he became rather . . . truculent. Regardless of whether he agreed with this behavior, it did not make Leeland happier to fight with his brother. And so he did his best to smooth things over. "I know we were both *thinking* the same thing about the water, in any case."

Laoch turned to him, and the eyes. Their gaze was fierce but profound—layers upon layers deep. "We're *twins*," Leeland whispered.

A swell of complicated feelings rose in Laoch's chest. His heart thumped beneath his amulet.

"Twins," he repeated.

"Alright you two, stop making out—" Nudge interrupted. "We've reached an impasse."

Before them a massive tangle of fallen trees crisscrossed the trail. Branches kinked at severe angles, forming tentlike cavities over the ground. And the webs—normally high above their heads—had been stretched by the collapsed timber so that a sticky white veil extended from the remaining canopy all the way down to the mess at their feet. It luffed gently in the breeze like a giant sail.

Because the felled trees were so tall, this eerie landscape continued for quite some time in either direction. It appeared there was no clear way around it. So they would have to go through it.

"No way. I'm not going in there," Sty said quickly.

"I'll have a look," Nudge offered. "Maybe it's not so bad." He stepped gingerly onto one of the branches and peered into the cave-like space it made with the ground. "Kind of dank in here," he commented.

"Do you see anything?" Leeland chirped nervously. He rather disliked Spiders as well.

"Not really." Nudge poked his head a bit farther in. "It's pretty dark in here, but—*AAARRGH!*" Something skittered over his forehead and he flopped backward, furiously wiping his face. "Get it off! Get it off!" he screamed.

"Hold still!" Laoch instructed, inspecting his friend's head. It looked perfectly normal, however, and though he assured him repeatedly that there was nothing there, Nudge continued for some time to comb through his fur.

Meanwhile, Sty was slowly backing away from the webbed wall before them, and Leeland poked the ground dejectedly with a stick. It appeared to Laoch that they were stalled out once again.

"Someone has to cut a path," he decided. He stomped his foot for emphasis.

The others looked up but said nothing.

I suppose Leeland's not as brave as everyone thinks, he mused. He rummaged through his pack for the hand scythe he'd brought along just in case they encountered a predicament such as this. He was good with the tool, having spent years clearing both wheat and windbush, a fibrous varietal his father cultivated on their land.

Laoch took to the tree pile unceremoniously. He detached the white webbing with precision, releasing sections to billow up into the air—enough so that he could pass beneath without becoming entangled. Then little by little he slashed a thin path through the twisted branches. Web. Branches. Web. Branches. Within the half hour, he had managed to clear a swath through the prickly morass and was just reaching the other side. The branches he cut he shoved into the tentlike hollows—not heeding the others' fears, but also not looking too deeply into the darkness.

"We're clear!" he called when he was almost through.

"You sure there's nothing in there?" Leeland yelled back. Even though Laoch had cleared a path, they would still have to climb past all those dark crevices.

"I'm sure!" Laoch shouted. But as he began to shove the last two sticks into a dark, hollow space beneath the branches beside him, he froze. There was, in fact, something there.

He had to blink to make sure he was seeing correctly, for it *was* extremely dim, and the shape crouched deep within the spiky cavern, away from daylight.

Two rows of eyes, glowing blackish green, shone out at him. And below, a black furry muff, from which hung two jagged, hairy fangs. Its long legs, pointed like spears, curled around a bulbous body.

"Okay, we're coming through!" Sty called nervously. He would have to climb with the others, as the hole Laoch cut through the webs was narrower than his wingspan.

Laoch heard them begin to pick their way through the bric-a-brac.

"Sounds good!" he yelled back, still frozen. He noiselessly adjusted his grip on the scythe. The Spider was at least twice his size.

As the boys' happy chatter drew closer, Laoch's panic increased.

Should I tell them? he thought frantically. *If they know it's here, they won't pass. And if they don't pass, we'll have to go back. . . .*

No, he decided, the monster mere feet from his face. *This is between you and me.*

"SPI-*DER*, SPI-*DER*, *WHERE–ARE–YOU*?!" Nudge sang playfully as they approached.

If you only knew, Laoch exhaled. He braced himself to strike at any moment. As the others reached him, he shifted so that his body obscured their view into the hollow. This left his midsection vulnerable, and he steeled himself for imminent evisceration.

"I'll meet up with you on the other side," he told them, trying to sound casual. "I'm just cutting a few more branches that I can sharpen into spears later on."

Not wanting to linger in the snag, the three shimmied past the last few boughs and popped out on the other side, back on the trail once again.

Meanwhile, the Spider made not a move.

If Leeland can survive that battle, Laoch thought, *and Nudge can kill a Bat . . . Well, I can take down this Spider.* But right then, the beast's fangs twitched, and he bolted from the trees.

"Run!" he yelled, pushing Nudge and Leeland ahead.

Without asking any questions they began to sprint down the trail, for there was already fear in their hearts. Even Sty was terrified, though from his high vantage point he did not see anything particularly the matter. Laoch looked back every now and then, but there was no sign of the Spider. So eventually, he slowed.

"What happened?!" Nudge exclaimed, out of breath once again. He didn't know if he could take much more running without replenishing their water.

"Nothing *happened*," Laoch lied. From the looks on his friend's faces, he knew there was no way he could tell them the truth. "I just wanted to get going. We were stalling for too long—"

"There was no need to scare us!" Leeland interrupted, clearly upset.

"No kidding," Nudge added dismally. "And what happened to your spears?"

Laoch sighed in exasperation. "It's just that we have to keep moving if we're ever going to make it to—"

"*UTOMIA. WE KNOW,*" both Leeland and Nudge replied together.

So the four trudged on, rather out of sorts. Laoch kept the scythe in his hand, peering behind them every few steps, just in case. But the Spider did not reappear, nor did any other dangers cross their path beyond their own silent exhaustion. Like this, the minutes turned to hours, until eventually the trail descended a hill. The boys rounded a sharp turn, when, lo and behold, they were led straight into a clearing. A hundred or so paces wide, the glade was padded with thick, spongy moss, a most iridescent green. The whole plot was completely enclosed by pines.

In the center was a clear pond lined with small, round rocks between which a spring vigorously fed. And from the pond ran a little stream that snaked through the mossy grove back into the forest.

Leeland dropped his pack and let out a sharp yelp.

Water.

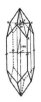

Chapter 24

WHEN A RABBIT HOPS BY

"What *is* this place?" Laoch breathed, too awe-struck to raise his voice above a whisper. Sty and Nudge stood beside him at the edge of the enchanting scene.

But Leeland had already scrambled into the clearing. He was surprised to find the moss so deep, and that his feet sprang up a bit with each step.

Step, *sproing!* Step, *sproing!*

In this manner the little Lizard, not usually one to make the first move, arrived at the pond ahead of all the others. He dove his head into the clean, clear water, gulping madly, the rest of his body prostrate on the ground.

Nudge, seeing this, gave a yelp of excitement and ran head-long into the moss garden, jumping and bouncing high into the air, a wild grin spread across his face.

"I'm flying!" he yelled, and shot high above the others, spreading his arms. He fell back in a swan dive to the spongy floor before launching up yet again. *"Weeeeeee!"* he howled, bounding toward the pond (for even his excitement over this bouncy new landscape did not erase his dire need for water).

After slaking his thirst, even Sty gave the moss a try. Since he was indeed the lightest of the four, he sprang up even higher than the others without having to beat his wings even once.

Laoch settled in at a far end of the grove, drinking from the stream that flowed through it. He watched as everyone jumped and bounded, and though he tried it a few times as well, he soon strayed off to explore. There were a few boulders covered in lichens and a darker strain of moss, which gave the impression that they'd been there for a very long time. And toadstools—huge ones! With thick white stalks bigger than his body and red-and-white speckled caps looming above his head. Underneath were other plants, and he recognized some of them: the lacey greenery of wild carrots and lettuce.

This place was not only a playground of giant propor-tion, he realized, but a source of food. Laoch felt his stomach rumble violently.

"Guys look, there's food here!" he called. The others' bouncing and frolicking immediately ceased, for they too were hungry—absolutely starving, in fact, as no one had eaten since the night before.

"Leeland, you dig up these carrots and anything else that looks good. Nudge, you scout for some berries and dry firewood. Sty, try to find some kind of meat—"

At Laoch's directives the boys sprang into action, and within a few minutes they were gathered in a circle around a small fire next to the pond. It wasn't cold enough to warrant a fire, but it comforted them to have one. They washed the vegetables that Leeland foraged, and the berries that Nudge picked, and set to eating voraciously until all of it was gone.

Sty hadn't had much luck scaring up any game, and Laoch, seeing that they'd already finished all the greens, was still hungry.

"What about the toadstools . . . do you think they're edible?" Nudge asked. He tapped one with his foot and watched it bob overhead.

"I don't know about that—" Leeland replied warily, racking his brain for any tips his mother might have passed along about cooking with wild fungal varieties. But Laoch was not so cautious. He had already begun to carve off large meaty chunks of mushroom stalk, tossing them to his friends.

"This is actually good!" Sty exclaimed, taking a dainty bite. (His mouth was not so big.) "Tastes like . . . like chicken."

*"Yeah, *tassshtes delisssshhhhious*," Nudge added, his mouth full of the stuff.

Leeland tentatively ate a little too, and seeing that nothing adverse seemed to be happening, finished his portion completely.

Laoch ate not one but two slabs of the mushroom and agreed that it did taste somewhat like chicken (although it was the kind of thing that one could get sick of quickly, which he did).

And so the four of them rested—Sty sprawled on the spongy moss, wings akimbo; Nudge lazily brushing his toes in the pond; Leeland staring up at the sky; and Laoch thinking to himself how nice it might be if a rabbit were to hop across the clearing.

As if by clockwork, another set of eyes peered out from behind a particularly large toadstool.

Laoch was the first to see the rabbit. It was pure white with red glossy eyes the size of saucers. He smiled to himself in disbelief, feeling he had somehow willed it into being. And what a Being it was: the rabbit was at least four times larger than himself or any of the others. How would they catch such a thing?

"Nudge! Sty! Leeland!" he whispered.

The rabbit blinked its eyes.

"Look over there! Behind that toadstool!"

Both Leeland and Nudge lifted their heads, their eyes widening with surprise.

"You've got to be kidding me—" Nudge gasped, scrambling to his feet. He was about to wonder out loud how the heck a rabbit grew so big when suddenly coming straight for them was an immense white face attached to an imposingly pale and silky body, followed by two powerful hind legs that would challenge in strength, Nudge surmised, even the most imposing of Hoppers.

The boys had no time to react to its movements, for it was so large—and the moss so spongy—that with only one bound it sprang forth from behind the towering mushroom stalk and its entire gleaming magnificence soared over their heads.

Sty, frozen with fear, remained glued to the moss (and in fact tried to sink into it farther so as to remain unnoticed by the massive creature).

Nudge, on the other hand, who was closest to where it touched down on the opposite side of the glade (for it had somehow leapt clean over the entire clearing), sprang into action. As the rabbit's hefty hind foot sunk into the moss, he lunged at it, throwing both of his arms around its ankle and screaming at the top of his lungs—for while being a very brave little Meerkat, he was also quite emotional and in this moment was truly scared for his life.

The rabbit whipped its head around. The boys (save Nudge, who was hanging on for dear life) shrank back, expecting rage or malice in its eyes.

But there was none.

Only fright, and the poor large animal started to quiver. It made another frantic leap. But this time, instead of heading into the forest—which would have been the better tactical move, as Nudge could have easily been scraped off its ankle on a tree trunk or stone—it bounded back over the boys in the direction from whence it appeared.

And as it did so, the most surprising thing happened.

Laoch watched Nudge as he sailed through the air still attached to the thing's ankle (screaming, his face a mixture of excitement and terror), and his mind raced, plotting his role in the rabbit's demise as soon as it landed—poor stupid, humungous animal that it was.

But Leeland—without so much as a word, or change of expression, or motion to stand (for like Sty he'd been paralyzed on his back throughout the whole ordeal)—reached his hand into his pack and pulled out the small cooking knife he'd taken from home. With a flick of his slender wrist he sent it spinning end over end just as the rabbit was sailing overhead, and both he and Laoch watched as the knife expertly lodged itself in its jugular.

As soon as the blade hit, a great flume of blood emerged starkly from the soft white fur, and the animal, instead of landing upright and absorbing the shock, fell full on its belly, its long hind legs dragging behind at full length.

Nudge, shaken, lay still for a moment, his arms still grasped tightly around the rabbit's leg. But soon he stood and poked the thing where it lay motionless, and presently took to jumping up and down excitedly.

"Look at what I did! I killed it!" he exclaimed. "I must have gripped its ankle . . . to *death*!"

He sprang around the moss, bouncing high over everyone's heads, doing a little victory dance in the air.

Laoch rolled his eyes.

"That was good . . . aim," he whispered to his brother (while ignoring Nudge, who continued to celebrate).

"I guess so."

"Did you not *see* what I just *did*?!" Nudge shouted, annoyed that the two of them were seemingly unimpressed by what was so obviously a miraculous feat.

"You didn't kill it," Laoch informed him. "Leeland did."

"What are you *talking* about, of course I killed it . . . I was holding it with a vice grip . . . the grip of a *thousand* Meer-kats, because when I get frightened . . . I mean, *excited* . . . my strength knows no bounds—"

"Look," Laoch said flatly. He moved to the head of the life-less rabbit, and with all his strength was able to lift it enough to reveal the bloody underside of its nape.

"Ewwwww!" Nudge squealed, leaping backward. They all knew he had a weak stomach when it came to blood.

"You hit it in the right spot," Sty observed. He always tried to catch rabbits in the throat. It lessened their suffering.

Leeland didn't say much of anything.

"It was a lucky toss, that's all," Laoch shrugged, the jealousy he felt little hidden in his tone. He tugged on the rabbit's ear, but it didn't budge. He wouldn't be able to move it alone.

"That's *all*?! Are you kidding me? It's incredible! It's a *MIRACLE*!" Nudge shouted, newly reenergized. "How did you do it? Did you have the knife on you already? How did you time it right? When did you learn how to throw like that?"

And then: "Have you ever *killed* something before?"

For although it was common for Sty to hunt all number of creatures, and both Nudge and Laoch had had some luck themselves with smaller vermin, they'd never known Leeland to take part in any hunting activities at all. He never *refused* to do it, they just never asked him to. It was as if they could sense he didn't have the constitution for it.

Which made this sudden move all the more baffling and incredible.

"I don't know, I don't know," Leeland muttered, shaking his head. "Let's just clean it and eat."

So they did.

The three boys, with great effort, dragged the corpse to the side of the grove while Sty gathered wood for a fire. Soon they began to clean the body, their arms and hands covered in blood. It was here that Leeland, reanimated, quietly helped the others find and remove the best meat. But if Leeland was the expert at all things culinary, Laoch was the master scientist. He commanded attention, speaking over his brother, and gestured authoritatively at all the different body parts while explaining in detail how each one worked. Nudge was fascinated and asked many questions, but Leeland was quiet and worked steadily. His cuts of meat were indeed the cleanest, which Nudge, again, commented on as being amazing. And though Laoch also gave him some accolades for this, he was slightly peeved that his brother seemed to have some kind of preternatural talent that in this circumstance surpassed his own.

Within an hour the deed was done, and they brought pounds upon pounds of fresh meat back to the fire. Nudge quickly foraged for some forked branches and stakes, and assembled a makeshift spit rotisserie from which they hung great strips of fresh, bright meat that began to crackle and hiss. An aroma such that none of the boys had ever smelled before circled around them. Sty even drooled a bit. Nudge, in order to distract himself while the meat cooked, took to reenacting the miracle of the rabbit's demise (with a decided focus on his own heroism, as well as Leeland's surprise skill with a weapon). But Leeland was still oddly silent. And Laoch, though happy to have the meat, was deep in thought as well, so surprised by his brother's feat.

It made him feel, for the first time in his life, that there were things about Leeland he didn't know. Or didn't understand.

But the others didn't bother with those thoughts, and they even cheered for him:

"Lee-*land*! Lee-*land*!" they yelled. Nudge picked him up for a moment and put him on his shoulder, though Leeland quickly wriggled down, shrugging off the whole thing.

"It's not that big of a deal, guys."

"Yeah, leave him alone. Any one of us could have killed that hare," Laoch added.

"But I didn't see *you* throwing any knives," Nudge teased, "or doing anything at all but sit there and watch!"

At this, Laoch tackled his furry friend, the two of them rolling around in mock battle.

Leeland and Sty watched with vague amusement, for they'd witnessed these shenanigans many times. Except that this time, the fighting seemed to last . . . a bit too long.

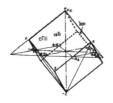

Chapter 25

KILLER

"I give up!" Nudge yelled.

But Laoch did not stop.

"I said I give up! LET ME GO!" the Meerkat shouted, baring his teeth. This he had never done before. Not to his friend. And as soon as he twisted out of Laoch's grip, he pounced away defensively.

Laoch stepped back, panting. "I'm sorry, I'm sorry—" he mumbled, but Nudge would have none of it.

"I don't know why you're fighting me when we all know you're just jealous of your brother!"

"What?"

"You heard me."

Nudge bounded off to the other side of the pond to nurse his injuries.

(They were mainly emotional, and therefore stung worse than any physical pains.)

"Come on!" Laoch called. "It's not that big of a deal."

Nudge didn't answer him.

"I said I'm sorry!"

Again, no response.

"Arrrgh," Laoch grumbled, turning to the others. They eyed him with what felt like pity. "Guess he can't take the heat—" he joked.

No one laughed.

"Oh come on, we were just messing around!"

Sty suddenly lifted off, as the whole thing made him quite uncomfortable.

This left the brothers alone.

Laoch plopped down on the moss next to Leeland. He would have done anything in that moment to take back his actions. To instead have merely said, "You're right, Nudge, I *didn't* do anything to kill the rabbit. And yes, Leeland *is* amazing." To have hugged his brother, asked if he was okay. For it had been such a long day. Such a long, harrowing day.

But even now, he couldn't bring himself to look at Leeland, never mind hug him. Something terrible prevented him from doing this. The thing Nudge had named, had let out into the open.

So instead, Laoch crossed his legs in front of the fire and tapped his brother on the knee. "Can you believe what Nudge *said*? What a crackpot," he said in an effort to diffuse the situation.

Leeland grunted in response, clearly not wanting to talk about it.

"Come on Lee, you're not vexed at me too, are you?"

Laoch hadn't called him Lee since they were Childlings. This touched Leeland's heart, but he was still upset. The young Lizard closed his eyes. Visions of the great rabbit falling from the sky, blood flying everywhere, repeated over and over in a continuous loop. This blurred into other visions—images of the battle. More blood, more noise. The sound of bones cracking, the last cries before death. Blood spray on his face, in his mouth.

He opened his eyes and stared into the flames. He gave the spit another good turn.

"Alright, Killer, suit yourself," Laoch muttered, standing abruptly. If no one wanted to talk to him, he might as well find something else to do.

"Don't *ever* call me that again," Leeland hissed. He jumped up and there were tears in his eyes.

"Listen Killer, if I knew you were so good with a knife I'd have put you out front the entire time—"

"I SAID, don't call me that!" Leeland repeated.

Laoch wanted to stop, but he couldn't. It was true. He *was* jealous of his brother. That Leeland had proven himself bravely, not once but many times on this journey. And this, amid so many of Laoch's own failings: his inability to find water, to lead them safely through the plains.

Why, you didn't REALLY even save them from the Spider, did you? that awful voice chimed in his skull.

He shook his head and shrugged, trying to silence it. "Alright, alright," Laoch conceded, raising his hands up in mock surrender. *"Geez . . . Just don't kill me next."*

With that, Leeland ran full bore at his brother. It was the only time he had ever done this in their whole lives. And it so surprised Laoch that he didn't even have time to jump out of the way. Leeland hit him square in the stomach with his shoulder, and Laoch flew backward onto the moss (which luckily proved to be a very soft landing). He wasn't hurt, but had a sick feeling in his gut nonetheless.

"Lee—" he began frantically. "Lee, I'm sorry!"

But Leeland, like Nudge, stalked off angrily.

"Lee!"

"LEAVE ME ALONE!" he screamed, disappearing behind a large toadstool at the other end of the clearing.

Laoch stood there a moment and looked around. The glade was utterly silent, save the trickle of the stream and the crackle of the fire. He scanned the entirety of the mossy grove, but the others were similarly hidden from view. *If they're even there at all*, he thought sickeningly.

"Looks like the meat is cooked!" he yelled, hoping this would rouse them.

No one stirred.

So he sighed and settled in next to the fire by himself. He slowly turned the spit until his arm ached (for the meat was hefty as could be), then turned it round some more. Eventually it was done, and he removed each piece with great care from the stake and piled them on a large flat rock. Though he was still hungry, he barely had the heart to take a bite.

For the first time since this journey began, Laoch was alone.

Nudge was the first to return to the fire. Dusk had begun to settle over the mossy grove and his overactive imagination—especially concerning ghosts and the like—overshadowed his hurt feelings. At first, he was rather standoffish and refused to address Laoch at all. But the jovial Meerkat hated conflict of any kind, and therefore it was all but impossible for him to hold a grudge. So, after a forthright apology—he'd requested that Laoch bow to him, which he did, and in turn *both* of them had a good laugh—Nudge was back to his old self, giggles and all. Plus, the meat was perfectly cooked, and Laoch had cut more slices of toadstool that soaked up the juices beautifully. With such a fine feast before them, it would be difficult to harbor ill feelings.

Sty was the next to join them. He'd been trying to satiate himself at the other end of the grove, munching on carrots and herbs. But his growing hunger and the smell of freshly cooked flesh finally got the best of him. And so, hearing that at least *some* of them were on speaking terms again, he winged over and helped himself heartily to the bountiful meal.

There was still a lot of food left, but the three of them were soon unable to sit up for they were so full. As they lay there looking up at the sky, dusk shifted to darkness throughout the mossy grove. The moon emerged, lending silvery edges to the scenery.

Sty—who would normally be waking at this hour after his midday sleep—began to doze.

"I don't know why I'm so tired," he yawned.

"It's from eating too much," Laoch replied, willing his eyes to stay open. He was terribly worried about his brother, but the others assured him that Leeland would come back when he was ready. It was just at that moment, in fact, when a soft, sweet voice came forth from the twilight:

"Guys, I can't get it out of my mind—"

Leeland appeared beside them.

"Let's put it behind us," Laoch whispered. "I'm so sorry I called you—"

"No, it's not that."

"Well if *I* were you I'd be thinking about it too," Nudge interrupted. "It's not every day that you successfully hunt a humungous rabbit with only one small knife . . . and one toss! Boy oh boy—"

"No, that's not what I mean," Leeland continued. "It's not just the rabbit. It's everything."

The other boys were silent then, for suddenly it dawned on them that since they'd entered the mossy clearing, the events from earlier in the day had become . . . harder to keep in one's head.

"What happened on the plains, all the blood—" Leeland started.

"We saw a Bat die," Sty whispered. Nudge put a paw on his shoulder.

"I'm sorry . . . I didn't even think about that . . . that it might make you feel . . . weird."

"It's okay. He was evil," Sty replied, though this was somewhat of a lie. For it *had* made him feel strange. Even though he was certain that the Bat, with its raggedy fur and razor teeth and seething eyes, would have killed them had Nudge not done so first.

"We both killed today," Nudge said to Leeland, who looked very sad and pulled his knees up to his chest.

"I know," he said quietly.

"Why don't you have something to eat," Laoch suggested. "That might make you feel better."

Leeland got himself a few bites of mushroom. He didn't have the stomach for rabbit anymore.

As Laoch watched his brother, his heart ached. He wanted to go to him, to comfort him. But the problem was, he could barely keep his eyes open. He blinked hard, willing them to see. It was then that he noticed something rather strange. Leeland's body began to emit a soft green light.

He turned to Sty, who was also glowing, though his light was orange. And Nudge's, a warm yellow.

He gazed down at his own body—his arms, his torso, his legs—and saw that he was radiating as well, a transparent but definitive indigo hue.

"Do you see this?" he whispered, but the others were already out cold. And so despite the fact that this was *quite* peculiar, and there was a gigantic Spider (possibly *many* of them) lurking in the trees just beyond their little grove, Laoch allowed his eyes to close as well. A tiredness like no other seeped through his limbs. His body sank into the moss as he drifted off, and he felt grateful, suddenly, for his very life. They had escaped imminent danger three times in the last few days. First in Talamh, then on the plains. And today in these very woods. And now, with the softest of surfaces below him, he felt thankful and amazed just to be there, and to be fed, and to be with his brother and two best friends.

As his body continued to melt into the deep moss, he imagined becoming one with it, slipping down through the tiny furls like water.

And like this, very quickly, he fell into a deep sleep.

Chapter 26

THE MIDDLE OF THE MIDDLANDS

L aoch woke with a start. His arms twitched, and he opened his eyes. Then closed them. Then opened them again, disoriented. Three-dimensional moonbeams lit down around him like translucent pillars, and every surface of the mossy grove was covered with crystalline sparkling light. He blinked again, wondering if he was in fact dreaming, for it was the most beautiful sight he had ever beheld.

The young Lizard propped himself up, surveying the sleeping bodies of his companions, when a strange feeling ran down his spine. The feeling that he was being watched. Still on the ground, he slowly turned around. . . .

"Ahhh!" he yelped.

There, behind him, was a giant toadstool that he *knew* was not there when he went to sleep. And not only that. The thing towered above his head, its thick stalk at least three times as wide as Laoch himself. The mushroom cap was at least twelve feet across. And atop *that* was the strangest thing of all. It caused him to slowly crawl backward, whispering to his friends:

"Leeland! Nudge! Sty! . . . Wake up! Please wake up!"

For on top of the mushroom cap sat a mammoth Hopper, quietly watching them with bulging eyes.

"Leeland! Sty!" Laoch hissed. He kicked Nudge with his foot, but the small Meerkat merely turned over, murmuring:

"Leave me alone, Laoch, I'm sleeping—"

"You really need to wake up. *All of you! Now!*"

With that, the other boys opened their eyes.

"What are you doing, Laoch, it's the middle of the night—" Leeland began, but then they saw it. Without so much as a word, the boys crawled toward one another, huddling together on the ground as if that would provide some kind of protection from their observer.

The Hopper, however, did nothing but continue to stare down at them.

Leeland calculated that it was at least ten times the size of Ms. Whakdak, who was a sizable lady to be sure, and he wondered briefly if all Beings in this woodland were larger than normal.

A soft beam of moonlight shifted over the Hopper's face, illuminating one of its eyeballs, which was not only light green, but opaque and unfocused.

Sty quivered and shrank behind Laoch while Leeland slipped behind Nudge, who was scrambling to get behind all the others, everyone vying for some kind of cover.

"Stop wriggling around like worms!" the Hopper said sharply, and they immediately froze.

"Wh-wh-wh-who are you?" Nudge stuttered.

"Inis Breag the Earnest," the Hopper replied.

Nudge started to giggle. It was a strange name, to be certain, but now was not the time for a giggling fit, and Laoch jabbed him in the ribs. This had no effect on the Meerkat, who—despite the instructions to stop wriggling around like worms—began to roll on the ground, trying to contain his laughter.

Leeland spoke up: "Please excuse my friend, Mister . . . er . . . I mean, Inis Breag . . . the Earnest. You see he has . . . well, sometimes . . . a kind of laughing . . . affliction."

"As do I," replied Inis Breag quite seriously, which made Nudge collapse with giggles all the more. Even Laoch cracked a smile, for Inis Breag did not seem like the laughing type.

Leeland—all of a sudden the conversationalist, Laoch thought—continued: "Would you mind, Sir, telling us where we are?"

"In the middle of the Middlands," he replied, his long tongue flicking over their heads to catch a great hairy-looking moth that was fluttering in a moonbeam.

This impressed the boys, and Nudge's laughter finally quieted into soft breathing, for one does have to catch one's breath after a giggling fit.

"Do you live here?" Sty asked Inis Breag, who had, other than his tongue, not really moved at all.

"I live where I am," Inis Breag replied.

As Laoch's eyes adjusted to the moonlight, he could make out more of the Hopper's face. It was as wide as the very toadstool on which he sat. His other eye was deep black and emerald green, in contrast to the milky one, and his rather dull skin was covered in tiny brown bubbles. So he presumed Inis Breag to be a Toad.

"What is this place?" Laoch asked then.

"Were you not listening the first time?" One of the Toad's brow bumps raised quizzically.

"Oh, the Middlands, yes. I meant . . . I suppose . . . what *are* the Middlands?"

"The Middlands are where you are," he responded flatly. One of his fronties twitched, then he resumed perfect stillness.

"And you are just passing through?" Sty queried, peeking out a bit from behind Leeland's back.

"You could say that," Inis Breag replied. "But I believe I should be asking, what are *you* doing here?"

The boys looked at one another and then back up at him.

"We're not exactly sure," Leeland began.

"We were running from . . . a battle," Nudge added.

"We followed a little path through the woods—"

"The Pineswitch Alley," Inis Breag corrected.

"Ummm, y-yes, th-that one," Laoch stammered. For someone just passing through, Inis Breag seemed to know an awful lot about the area. "We're just camping here for the night. We're on a journey."

"I know."

The boys glanced at one another again, this time more apprehensively.

"How do you know, Sir, if you don't mind me asking?" Lee-. land uttered bravely.

"I know all things," Inis Breag replied.

"Then you are—" Nudge started, but Inis Breag cut him off.

"Never mind that. Have you any meat left? I can"—he flicked his tongue into the air—"smell it."

I always forget that some Hoppers can smell with their tongues, Laoch thought. He stepped toward the rest of the rabbit they'd been unable to finish before they fell asleep. "Yes we do! Lots! Do you want some?"

"No no," Inis Breag said with an air of disgust. "I never touch the stuff. It interferes with my thinking."

"Your thinking?"

"My way of knowing, you see."

The boys were beginning to understand that Inis Breag the Earnest and his way of knowing were perhaps more abstruse than they were accustomed to.

"Well . . ." Nudge began, but trailed off. He didn't really know what to ask of Inis Breag, nor what he might want with the boys.

"You'd like to know your fortunes, you say?" Inis Breag stated finally, flicking his tongue out once again, this time right past Sty's face, where it attached—sticky, as it was—to another fluttering moth. Sty thought he heard a miniscule shriek come from the insect as it was caught. All four of the boys watched the tongue expertly retract in one giant curl back into the Hopper's mouth.

"Well, I suppose—" Nudge said.

"You either *do* want to know, or you *don't* want to know," Inis Breag replied. "Most Beings prefer the latter."

This annoyed Laoch.

"Well, we *do* want to know," he announced rather testily, and the milky green eye of Inis Breag the Earnest blinked.

"Do you know how a soothsayer such as myself *works*, my boy?"

"Of course I do," Laoch replied. He did not.

"Very well. I'll do yours first. Others, please step away from your little green friend."

Leeland, Nudge, and Sty backed away slowly, and Laoch shrugged, shooting them a grin as if to say: "Can you *believe* this guy?" when Inis Breag's long, sticky tongue shot out from his mouth, wrapped itself around Laoch's waist, and hoisted him into the air.

"Hey! Stop!" he screamed, wriggling his arms and legs every which way. This was in vain, however, for the tongue was strong and thick and very tacky, and there was no way he was getting free until Inis Breag decided it was time.

"Ssthhooppp mooovthing," Inis Breag the Earnest lisped, *"I neeeed tooo connttthhhenntrate!"*

Nudge began giggling again, and even Leeland and Sty cracked smiles at Laoch's furious expression. For he was rendered completely helpless and was embarrassed too to be caught in such a position. But, nevertheless, he did quiet his thrashing and within a few moments the tongue brought him back down to the mossy ground, unwrapped itself from his body, and retracted into the Toad's mouth.

"Pure light," Inis Breag said, "casts the biggest shadow."

No one said anything for a moment. Laoch ran the words over in his mind, trying to puzzle it out. But it made no sense at all. He wasn't a light. He had a shadow, to be sure, but so did everyone else.

"What does that mean?" he asked finally.

"I never said I was an *interpreter* of fortunes," Inis Breag replied. "You'll have to find Branic the Wild for that. Who's next?"

Nudge, the bravest of the remaining three, stepped forward, for he was actually somewhat excited to get lifted into the air by a giant tongue. And so Inis Breag repeated the process, and Nudge was hoisted up and soon replaced on the ground.

"You shall live a life of deception! Take care!"

At this, Nudge's easygoing smile drained from his face.

"But I never lie!" he replied indignantly. "I mean, I don't tell really *big* lies. . . . I mean of *course* I lie to my parents sometimes, about what I've been up to or where I've been, but those aren't really *lies* per se, more just a smoothing over of the truth. . . . I would *never* lie about something serious, I mean if it was *really* important—"

"Who's next?" Inis Breag interrupted, and this time Sty stepped forward shyly.

"I'll go," he said, and again, Inis Breag lifted the boy up with his tongue for a few moments, then let him go.

"Brotherhood conquers all."

Laoch stepped forward a little aggressively, putting his arm around Sty. "We already *know* that. We're *all* brothers here . . . in spirit, anyway," he told the Hopper.

Inis Breag disinterestedly turned to the side and belched. A terrible smell quickly enveloped the boys, and all of them gasped and covered their noses.

"I suppose that leaves you," he said, fixing the milky eye on Leeland, who indeed felt apprehensive about the whole thing. He didn't want to be wrapped up in the Toad's tongue. The thought of it, in fact, made him a bit queasy. And now, with that terrible, terrible smell . . .

Leeland stepped forward in order to tell Inis Breag that he didn't want to get his fortune told—"You see, Sir, I'm not really the sort who wants to hear that kind of thing"—but before he could finish the tongue was out, and he was wrapped up in it, and found himself dangling almost ten feet above the ground, feet swinging free.

Laoch and the others waited for him to be placed back on solid ground, as everyone had after a few minutes, but this seemed to be taking longer. Inis Breag the Earnest closed his eyes and squinted them shut tight, causing all number of wrinkles to appear around his face. He coughed, and some moth dust was spewed into the air, lit by moonlight. Sty groaned, as did Nudge.

"What's taking so long?" Laoch demanded. As the minutes passed and he watched his brother continue to be suspended by the Toad's sticky tongue, he felt he should intervene.

"Let him go!" Laoch yelled up at them.

"Hooolllddd onnn, I'm thhhinnnthking," Inis Breag lisped, before finally putting Leeland down and opening his eyes.

"You shall seal your fate with leather."

A huge smile spread over Leeland's face and he turned to the others. "Get it?" he said excitedly.

Nudge giggled. "It's your *c-c-c-cobbling!*" he exclaimed, breaking into full belly laughs.

"It's the only one that makes any sense!" Sty added.

But Laoch shook his head, unimpressed. "Your fate shall be sealed with leather," he muttered under his breath, thinking that Inis Breag the Earnest was even more of a kook than he originally supposed.

The Toad, however, didn't seem amused by the boys' reactions to his fortunes and went back to his sleepy silence as he stared down at them.

"Are you just going to stare at us all night?" Laoch asked, hoping he'd leave.

"Yeah, I thought you were just passing through," Sty added.

"I believe we are all just passing through," Inis Breag replied. "Didn't you say you were on a journey?"

"*We're* going to Utomia!" Nudge exclaimed, recalling their purpose (which had seemed further and further from his mind ever since entering the mossy grove). But now that he remembered their mission, or so he thought, his body filled with restive energy and he bounced around on the moss to calm his nerves.

"Then you must be going soon," Inis Breag professed, blinking hard. "Best to travel in the moonlight."

"We'll go by morning," Laoch said authoritatively.

"Suit yourself," Inis Breag replied, suddenly rearing a bit. The boys watched as he, almost in slow motion, hopped off the toadstool, which bent and swayed under the force of his legs. Inis Breag landed in the moss next to them, and they could see now that he was at least four times as tall as they. "But I would always travel in the moonlight, if you want to get where you're going."

"That doesn't make any sense," Laoch shot back, hoping that Inis Breag would just leave them alone once and for all.

"Oh but it does. For the moonlight guides all of us, whether we know it or not. It reflects on lichens. The northerly type. Have another bite of my toadstool stalk, and you shall see."

The boys, unsure of what he meant, said nothing. But Leeland, closest to their food pile, snatched up a slab of uneaten mushroom, took a bite, and passed it along to the others. Laoch grimaced, for he was sick of the stuff . . . and moreover, was sick of Inis Breag the Earnest.

The Toad, however, waited patiently for the boys to eat, then pointed toward the pines on the edge of the clearing. Right before their eyes, some of the moss, illuminated by moonbeams, sparkled blue and green in a shimmering pathway that was previously not there at all.

"A path!" Leeland exclaimed. "Do you see it?"

The others nodded, but Inis Breag continued: "Of course I see it, I just showed it to you." With that he took another hop, heading toward the trail that had just appeared.

"Where are you going?" Nudge cried. If he could make pathways appear like that, maybe he could set them on their way to Utomia. "Can you show us the way out of the forest? Or through the plains to Utomia?"

Inis Breag the Earnest hopped again.

"The moonlight will show you—"

"Wait!" Leeland cried suddenly. "I have one more question!"

The Toad hopped away from them a third time, letting out a loud fart as he landed in the cushy moss.

"One too many, that is," Inis Breag murmured.

"My parents," Leeland went on. He scrambled to catch up with the Toad. "Can you tell us *their* fortunes? Please Sir, it's very important—"

"I most certainly cannot," Inis Breag belched over his shoulder.

"Please," Leeland pleaded. "They were kidnapped and we don't know where they are!"

Now at the very edge of the clearing, Inis Breag languidly scratched his enormous white belly with one long, crooked toe. His tongue unfurled and then retracted. He seemed to hum a little song.

"I repeat, not for my own health but because you cannot seem to comprehend, that I *cannot* tell your parents' fortunes."

Leeland hung his head, but Laoch breathed a sigh of relief. He'd rather maintain that they were still alive. That they'd be okay at the end of all of this. For if he didn't, there would be no reason to go on.

"But I will say," the Toad added, still humming intermittently, and in an oddly high tone wholly unfitting of his voluminous gullet, "that they are in a terrible way. A *terrible* way, I assure you."

"What?!" Leeland exclaimed as the Toad advanced down the sparkling path. "What do you mean?"

But Inis Breag did not turn, and did not stop. *"Pooooor souls, pooooor souls,"* he hummed under his breath as he took one last long leap and disappeared into the dark woodlands beyond.

And just like that, the four boys were alone once again.

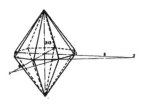

Chapter 27
BY THE LIGHT OF THE MOON

"Get everything together," Laoch instructed, already packing up his things. Nudge hurriedly refilled their canteens (for it appeared he'd finally learned his lesson), and Sty hastily wrapped some meat in an extra jacket and stuffed it into a bag.

"Laoch," Leeland implored. "What do we *do*?" The poor little Lizard was so upset by the Toad's foreboding words that he could not yet move a muscle.

"We get out of this crazy place," Laoch replied soberly, tossing him his pack. "We forget everything that crackpot said." He tightened his straps, scythe in hand. "And we get ourselves to Utomia. *Now*."

And so the boys left the mossy grove forever—with its spongy floor and oversized mushrooms, its gurgling pond, and its beams of moonlight so strong and pillar-like that they might as well have been made of alabaster stone.

The others followed Laoch across the grove until they reached the pine forest where Inis Breag had disappeared. The shimmering pathway he took had also vanished, so Sty flew in front as he was better at navigating in the dark. Though the threat of Spiders was on everyone's mind—especially Laoch's—no one breathed a word about it. And though progress was somewhat slow, within the hour they emerged out the other side, back on the plains. As they stepped out from the darkened wood, they spied a scene both unexpected and magnificent. For in the wide-open prairie, the moon hung over them directly, igniting the topography in soft light. As before, the grasslands stretched on as far as the eye could see, but what lay in front of them in the foreground was truly eerie. For the fallen bodies of those lost in battle remained half lit, and loomed large and deathly still like misshapen boulders.

"*Oh—*" Leeland gasped. No one moved, each taking it in.

"Do you think it's safe?" Nudge asked, and Sty took to the air.

"I'll check it out," he called, and the others watched him fly above the bodies, circle, and return.

"They're all—" he began, but didn't finish. He didn't need to. Everyone knew they were dead.

"Which way do we go now?" Nudge asked. They had pursued Inis Breag the Earnest but never found him, and now they were without a plan or a path.

Yet just as the words came out of his mouth, a warm breeze gusted toward them, sweeping the grasses into undulating waves. On the ground, little multicolored trails of phosphorescent lichens shot out from where they stood in all directions, moving like electricity and continuing onward into the distance.

"Whoa! Do you see that?!" Leeland exclaimed. "Which one do we follow?"

"I don't know," Laoch said. "Let me think for a minute." And he did, puzzling over how Inis Breag might have gotten just *one* path to ignite. While he thought, the others remained silent, transfixed by the colored patterns that were spreading throughout the gray grasses all around them. Warm, soft winds of the night continued to swell and blow against their faces, the ominous but strangely beautiful forms of the dead looming not so far away.

"We've got to do this," Laoch muttered, breaking the silence. "We've got to get to Utomia." As soon as the words were out of his mouth, however, the lights changed. He would have sworn the moon pulsed brighter for a moment (though he kept this observation to himself, as it seemed almost as crazy as Inis Breag and his fortunes). Still, the twinkles on the ground changed, and many were extinguished altogether. Others bent to join each other, coalescing into one strong band leading straight through the land of fallen soldiers, then gently curving to the left in the distance beyond.

"I see it!" he said, astonished.

The others exclaimed too:

"How did that happen?"

"Do you think that's the way?"

"Why didn't this happen the night we were with Mr. Moongate?"

"It's the mushroom, stupid."

"I think it's because of Inis Breag the—"

"Forget about him. C'mon! Let's go!"

While no one could say with any kind of certainty *why* they could suddenly see these glittering pathways, it didn't matter. Laoch set off in front, followed by Nudge, then Leeland, while Sty flew alongside.

The pathway was almost like a living thing too, for it did not remain stagnant and idle. Rather, it shimmered in and out of visibility, only to reappear farther up ahead. Still, Laoch and the others marched on. And when it disappeared for more than a few minutes, he would whisper—*"Utomia, Utomia"*—and like magic the lines would reappear, stretching in soft curves through miles of grass. The winds shifted and carried them along, rushing sweet-smelling air around their determined steps. Moonbeams scattered around the fields in silver strands. Here and there soft gray clouds dotted the black of the sky. No longer talking, each boy was lost in his own separate thoughts and sensations. They would rise over knolls and crests, then dip into subtle valleys only to emerge again on another series of hills, the glittering lines of phosphorescence leading the way.

After some time, Laoch lost track of how far they had traveled. He watched the shimmering trails come and go. Being in the lead, he felt great responsibility in guiding his brother and friends through unknown territory. His heartbeat grew more pronounced as they moved on. Now and then he would touch his amulet, the one his father gave him, and feel his pulse quicken. Or reach into his pocket to make sure that the golden disc was still safely tucked inside.

What he could not see, however, was that Leeland, bringing up the rear of this motley train, would also reach for his amulet from time to time. He felt a similar strength gathering within him. He held his breath every few steps just to make sure he was still in control of his own body, for the sensations he was experiencing were very odd indeed.

Shivers on his skin.

Warmth in his chest.

And strangest of all: he began to think he was seeing things.

Not just the strange glowing lichens on the ground, nor the moonbeams, nor the scattered gray clouds, nor the shadowed waves of grass around them.

But a golden eminence, rising in the distance.

He kept this observation to himself for a bit, and they continued in silence, save the *swoosh* of footfalls through the grass. But as the minutes passed, the distant aura of light grew stronger, and finally he spoke up.

"Do you see that? Up ahead?"

"What?" Nudge whispered, reaching for the knife he'd tucked into his belt after the rabbit incident (hoping he'd have a chance to kill a giant rabbit too, since it had seemed incredibly warrior-like when Leeland did it).

"There's a sort of glow coming from beyond that rise."

Leeland pointed, and the others stopped and looked. Laoch realized that he'd been so focused on following the shifting pathways that he hadn't looked up at the horizon much at all. But indeed, there was a glow, and upon seeing it his heart thumped inexplicably.

"Aw, that's just the sun coming up," Nudge stated knowingly.

"Nudge, the sun comes up in *that* direction." Leeland pointed east.

"Oh yeah," Nudge said, a little embarrassed. "I knew that."

Meanwhile, Sty flew up into the air without a word. His whisper of a body beat against the night wind.

"It's there! The city! We made it!"

Upon hearing this, the others broke into a run, their sacks thudding against their backs and legs. They covered ground quickly, not caring anymore about the glittering trails. With each footfall a shock of lights emanated, haphazardly criss-crossing in shifting patterns of electric pink and orange and blue. As they neared the crest of the rise, their hearts beat as they never had before—not in play, nor escaping Talamh, nor fleeing the battle on the plains. A sight more magnificent than all of their shared imaginings appeared inch by inch before their eyes until they stopped at the very top of the ridge. Speechless and awestruck, they gazed down at what lay in the distance below them.

Utomia.

Chapter 28
ALL FOR ONE,
AND ONE NOT AT ALL

Once the boys started running, they didn't stop. As the first signs of a rising sun issued from the east, the great city emerged in front of them, a shining orb in the middle of the plains. At the sight of it, Laoch knew he would never be too surprised at anything ever again. And though the worst had already happened, and his parents were taken away, and none of them knew anything about where they were or how they'd fared, Laoch did know one thing for certain. It rang through his thoughts and body and his very heart as he ran:

I've made it this far, and I'll make it the rest of the way too, whatever that takes. I'll get my parents back, safe and sound.

Every few minutes he would look back to make sure the others were keeping pace. Now it seemed more important than ever to stay together.

They moved so swiftly that Leeland, Laoch worried, would drop behind. But every time he whipped around to check, there he was, not three feet astern. Laoch could be sure of this too, because every now and then Leeland's cobbling belt would flap up and then slap back down against his hip with a decided *snap*.

Nudge, only a few steps back, ran with singularity of emotion. His face was fierce, as Laoch imagined it might be right before a Water Games competition, were he to make it that far. The long rushes of reeds and grasses dried from days baking in the hot sun fell away from Nudge's legs, his muscles turning over with sustained determination.

Sty swooped around them like a swallow in what Laoch could only perceive as joy, for he was usually such a somber little fellow. *The sweetest of us all*, he thought, realizing that the loyalty and love of Sty in particular was miraculous, given the terrors of the past few days and what they had learned about the rest of Batkind.

As they advanced upon the city it only grew larger, and taller, and more fantastic until finally they were only a few hundred feet from the massive stone wall enclosing it. Here the boys stopped, their mouths agape. The domed roof of Utomia rose high above the plains like a giant bubble.

The Water Shield, a thing to behold, glinted in the now fully risen sun. Beyond it, the sprawling metropolis—all angles of stone and spear pointing to high heaven and beyond—shimmered through water. A distant tower in the center of the city stood taller than the rest, almost a mile high and punctuating the horizon not unlike the purple smoke cloud they had left behind.

The stories they'd heard about this place were true.

"I can't believe it, I just can't believe it," Nudge breathed, still recovering from their long run.

Sty spun through the air in an ecstatic corkscrew. He too was filled with hope. This was a new feeling for him, and it overtook his entire being more strongly, even, than had the seductive callings of the Other Bats. The city was almost too beautiful to behold, and because of this he instantly believed that anything they'd find inside such a magnificent place would be good.

"It goes on for *miles!*" he exclaimed, his wonderment reflected in the eyes of his companions.

"We're going to get inside," Laoch told the others resolutely. As if all of them didn't implicitly believe the same, they nodded obediently, for despite all that had happened he was still very much their leader.

"I bet there are all sorts of swell things in there," Nudge added, the four now plodding ahead in a tight group. The distance remaining between them and the metropolis diminished with every step. "I heard they have weird contraptions that fly and move all on their own, and little glass bulbs that light up the room instead of candles—"

"What they have in there is the key to the meaning behind *this*," Laoch interrupted, pulling out the golden disc his father had given him and flashing it in front of his friends. It reflected impressively in the sun.

Leeland saw for the first time what a beautiful object it was. He blinked in the harsh light, and a momentary hollow feeling passed over him as he realized that it was given to Laoch alone. His father neglected to find something important for him. *No matter*, he consoled himself quietly. *I can still help rescue them, in my own way.* (Though he wasn't quite sure what way that was.)

The city was now only a few paces away. The boys could see various doors along the surrounding wall, and figures standing guard.

"Looks like we'll have to go through those blokes," Nudge said wearily. "I hope they're nothing like *Inis Breag the Earnest*."

Leeland groaned, remembering the strange Toad, but Sty reminded them that he had set them on their way to Utomia.

"I still wonder what our prophesies meant. Do you think there's any truth to them? I wonder if they can help us get into the city somehow . . ." he mused, flying low to the ground. He had been thinking about his a lot—*Brotherhood conquers all*—and what it might mean. The obvious and first thought he had was that it referred to his friends, for they were the only brothers he'd ever known, even though they weren't blood related. Even though he had Other Status, and they did not. But then again, in the days since the invasion he'd felt another strange kind of brotherhood, not that he'd thought about it in those terms. It was more of a nagging sensation. . . .

Still, any connection he'd felt to the Other Bats, wanted or unwanted, now fell away. His heart was alight with excitement and pride. For they had crossed the Great Plains, together. And faced possible death, together. And now would enter the famed city, all of them side by side as brothers.

And so, feeling closer to his friends than he ever had before, Sty snuggled against Nudge's back, tucking himself into the carrying sack.

"When we get there, let me do the talking, okay?" Laoch instructed.

"What, you don't trust us?" Nudge shot back, a decided spring in his step as he thought up some funny lines he might say to whomever was guarding the entryway.

"Well maybe the other two, but certainly not you." Laoch grinned. Nudge stuck out his tongue and skipped ahead, but Laoch overtook him and motioned for the others to stay back.

In this way, with Laoch in the lead, the four weary travelers approached an arched entryway in the Wall. It was ten or twelve feet wide, twenty feet in depth (a very thick wall indeed), and almost double that in height. Laoch noted that about halfway through the entryway, the Water Shield rose from the ground and extended to the top of the arch, filling the opening completely.

He also noted two Guards—one male, one female, both Lizards—standing on either side. They appeared to be around Laoch's age—perhaps a year or two older at most—which instantly bolstered his confidence. Why, the Utomians had mere teenagers guarding the city! They were nothing like the fearsome warriors they had seen on the plains.

As Laoch approached them, the female rested her hand on the handle of a thin but very sharp-looking blade that hung from her belt. The other Guard's posture was more relaxed, and Laoch detected what could only be a slight smile upon his lips.

The choice was very simple about whom to address first.

"You guys stay here," Laoch whispered to his friends, and was about to introduce himself when Sty, still clinging to Nudge's back, propped himself up on a wing and craned around to see what was going on.

Both Guards immediately drew their weapons.

"STAY BACK!" the female shouted. The male Guard took a threatening step in their direction. Both of their expressions were fixated on Sty, who shrank back and let out a small shriek.

Of course, Laoch thought, realizing what was happening.

He put his hands up and stepped toward the Guards, who advanced upon him defensively.

"Stay where you are, fella," the male Guard instructed forcefully.

"Come no farther," the female Guard added, pointing her sword in Laoch's direction.

But Laoch did not listen. Rather, he took another step.

"It's not what you think—"

"I said NO FARTHER!"

"He's a Kindly Bat! We're from the Southern Hills.... I *swear* to you.... Look at us, we're just teenagers.... We were forced to flee.... *PLEASE* put down your swords!"

The male Guard tentatively lowered his weapon, but the female kept hers drawn.

"Prove it," she said in a steely voice.

"Ummm," he mumbled, glancing back at the others. He wished they would stop cowering, for it made them all look guilty. Still, Laoch had no idea how to prove that Sty was a Kindly Bat.

"How do we do that?" he asked. "I mean, I've already sworn to you—"

"I don't think you realize how serious this is," the female Guard continued. She was encroaching with her pointy sword.

"I . . . I . . . I don't have the mark," Sty squeaked, still hiding.

"What are you *talking* about?" Nudge hissed under his breath. He was not especially keen that the object of the Guards' attention was strapped to his body. *"What mark?"*

"Sty, please just let me handle—" Laoch began, but was cut short as the little Bat, quivering with fright, shot out from behind his furry friend and turned around, revealing his backside. It was solid in color—a deep, soft gray. The female Guard reluctantly lowered her sword, keeping an eye on him all the same.

"The Trazo Blano," she murmured knowingly. "He doesn't have it."

Sty returned to his carrying sack and burrowed against Nudge, who was quite confused.

"What is she talking about?" he whispered.

"The mark of the Other Bats," Sty's voice wavered. "I saw it when they invaded Talamh—"

The Guards looked at each other.

"You're from *Talamh*, you say?" the female inquired.

"Yes, we fled—" Nudge explained.

"We've been traveling this whole way alone," Leeland added. "It's been *terribly* difficult, and we're *awfully* tired, and we just want to get into the city to rest for a spell, so if you'd be so kind—"

But the Guards ignored him.

"How did you manage to escape?" they asked suspiciously.

Laoch couldn't believe his ears. This conversation was going exactly how he'd hoped it wouldn't.

"We slipped out near the edge of town," Sty said quietly, "while the Other Bats were investigating the smoke—"

"Smoke? What do you know about the smoke?" the male Guard demanded. All six of the young Beings gazed south where still, very clearly, a thick purple column was stamped against the brilliant morning sky.

"Nothing, nothing," Laoch said quickly. "We don't know anything about the smoke." He shot the others a withering look. He'd told them to let him handle things, and now look what had happened. "Can we please start over?" he stammered. "My name is Laoch."

"And you think we care what your name is *because* . . ." the male Guard retorted with an impertinent sneer. The female Guard shot her cohort an annoyed look that made Laoch wonder if they weren't in fact on the best of terms.

"We just want to stay for a bit, until we can go back home," he tried, but they would have none of it.

"Listen, buddy," the male Guard grumbled. "I don't know who you think you are . . . *Loo-kak*, or *Lum-back*, or whatever your name is. But just so you get the picture, you can't just '*stop by*' Utomia for a visit."

His tone was sarcastic. Laoch disliked him.

"It's *Laoch*," he corrected.

"You should probably move on," the female Guard added. "There's a town a few days' walk from here." She pointed west.

Crestfallen, Laoch gazed off into the great wide nothingness. The thought of setting out into the plains again was almost too much to bear, for they had come so far. His friends huddled behind him, their faces drawn with disappointment. He couldn't let them down. He couldn't let his *parents* down. Not now.

"But there's got to be some kind of protocol for entering the city, right?"

The Guards shared an uneasy look.

"There are a series of . . . *tests*, I guess you could say," the female began.

"Enchantments," the other added in a feigned spooky voice, wiggling his stubby green fingers as if making fun of their whole situation.

"Shut up Roz," the female Guard hissed. "Sorry about that. My colleague here likes to joke around. But I assure you this is no joking matter."

"Can we try to pass the tests or what?" Laoch asked, feeling more and more frustrated with the two of them.

"Wellll—" she started.

"You know they're allowed to *try*," the male Guard said to her quietly. It was an aside, but Laoch could hear every word. "I mean, *any* Being can try . . . it's not like they'll get *in*."

"I know," she huffed. This irritated Laoch even more, them speaking as if he couldn't hear. But he pretended not to notice and kept his mouth shut.

"Okay," she stated finally. "You can try. And when ... I mean ... *if* ... you don't get through, you'll have to leave. *Immediately.*"

"We promise!" Laoch replied, and turned around. "What do you think, boys? You ready to explore this great city?!"

The others appeared less excited than they'd been before meeting the taciturn Guards. "Yeah, we're ready," they mumbled.

"Approach the archway," the female Guard instructed. Laoch motioned for the others, still in a huddled mass, to join him.

But all was not well.

"NOT THAT ONE!" Roz barked harshly. He pointed his sword toward Sty, who had advanced with the others.

Sty darted off, landing on the ground just a few yards away. He looked very small and very frightened against the backdrop of the plains.

"But he's one of us!" Nudge pleaded. "We can't leave him!"

"Please, I don't think you understand—" Laoch explained, turning to the female Guard.

"No, I don't think *you* understand. There are absolutely NO Bats allowed in the city. I don't *care* if he's a Kindly Bat." She turned to Sty, her stance immobile. "I'm very sorry, whoever you are, but you cannot come near Utomia. It is just the way of things."

The way of things is wrong, Laoch thought vehemently, and clenched his fists.

"But where will you *go*?" Leeland cried.

"I don't know," Sty replied meekly. He edged little by little away from the others. Even though the Guards had already squashed the happy feelings he'd had upon arriving at the city, he still harbored hope that everything would work out as they'd planned. But now, exposed and shunned, the little Bat's heart closed up again. *Brothers,* he thought sadly. The illusion was shattered and there was nothing anyone could do about it.

"I'll go back to Talamh," he said. "Don't worry about me. It won't take me longer than a day or two. I'll wait for you there. I'll send news from home."

It struck the others, then, that Sty could have flown all the way to Utomia in a fraction of the time it took them to trek across the plains.

"But it's *dangerous*—" Leeland warned, on the verge of tears.

Sty just shook his sorry little head. "No . . . not for me."

"But we need to stick together!" Laoch insisted. He looked at Sty, then at the Guards, then back at Sty, then back at the Guards. "Isn't there *any* way we can work this out?"

Leeland and Nudge silently implored their winged friend, unsure of what to do. "If Sty doesn't get in, then *I* don't get in,"

Nudge announced suddenly. He tried to put his arm around him in solidarity, but Sty held up a wing, staving him off.

"Go," he said. "It's the only way you'll find what you need." In his voice there was rare resolve that no one dared question, even Laoch. Deep down, they knew he was right.

And so the others woefully turned their backs on him to face the Guards, who were growing impatient.

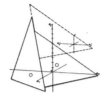

Chapter 29

TO BE SEPARATED BY
A THIN SHEET OF WATER

"Approach the archway," the female Guard repeated. She pointed at three circles on the ground beneath the hood of the giant portal. Laoch didn't remember seeing those before. As he, Leeland, and Nudge stepped forth, he also noticed the intricacy of her tattoos, the largest depicting a splash of water that spread from underneath her tunic up the back of her neck.

"What are your names?"

The boys told her.

The male Guard, whom she'd addressed as Roz, held his palm up to one of the gray stones in the Wall. Its color changed, and a series of small beeps and then three or four unseemly *HONKS* rang out. Roz shook his head.

"Stupid thing never works," he muttered.

Neither of the Guards seemed impressed at what was happening to the rock, but to the boys it was a fantastic illusion the likes of which they'd never seen before.

Underneath Roz's palm, the stone grew transparent as apple jelly, revealing the inner workings of electrical nerves. A matrix of sorts, it shimmered in its own furious rhythm. Almost immediately the circles upon which each boy stood—nothing more than drawings in the sand—grew distinct and metallic. Holographic columns of light beamed down from the top of the archway and surrounded their bodies. Each was a different color: Leeland's green, Nudge's yellow, and Laoch's a deep indigo hue.

Sty gasped, watching from afar.

"Don't move," the female Guard instructed, "or you'll upset the scanners." She paced around the light beams encapsulating the boys. "We're going to ask you a series of questions. Nod if you would like to proceed."

They nodded.

"You can all answer at the same time, don't worry about taking turns," Roz added. Clearly they had done this before.

"Is your name Laoch?"

"Yes."

"No."

"No."

The scanners blinked.

"Is your name . . . Looktok?"

Nudge giggled, despite himself.

"No."

"No."

"No."

They blinked again.

And so on. Once each had been asked whether his name was or was not his name, or some variation thereof, Roz continued.

"Are you connected in any way with Olc or the Other Army?"

"No," they replied together.

The lights flickered around them.

"Are you from Talamh?"

A resounding: "Yes."

"Are your intentions here true and pure?"

This was a harder question. *That's sort of subjective*, Laoch considered silently, and Roz spoke again, this time in a stronger tone:

"Are your intentions here TRUE and PURE?"

"Yes!" Leeland responded quickly.

"Yes?" Nudge spoke, not sounding sure of himself at all.

Both of their scanners blinked.

"I think it's a subjective question," Laoch began slowly. He thought about what his intentions in fact *were*. At this exact *moment* his main intention was to find the meaning behind the disc his father had given him, so that somehow he might rescue his parents from their captors. And nothing, to Laoch, seemed more true and pure than that. "But yes, my intentions are true and pure."

HONK HONK HONK went the mechanism.

Roz shook his head and kicked the Wall. Almost immediately the beam surrounding Laoch blinked, and then all three light columns vanished as quickly as they had appeared.

"Is that it? Can we go through?" Laoch asked. The Water Shield was but a few feet in front of them, flowing freely across the entryway.

"Not quite," the female Guard replied sardonically. She approached the Wall and placed her hand on a different stone. Sure enough, it instantly turned translucent and full of strange circuitry. She adeptly pressed the glowing, holographic buttons in a complicated pattern. "This is the last part," she continued, suddenly taking Laoch's hand into hers.

As soon as their skin touched, he startled. A cool electric shock ran up his arm to the top of his head, then down the back of his neck. Little goose bumps formed all over. His cheeks grew hot, and he pulled his hand back.

"What's wrong with you?" she grumbled, grasping for him again. She led him to the Water Shield, and positioned his face only inches away from the rushing stream of water. It was somewhat akin to a waterfall, and Laoch could smell the unmistakable scent of water on hot stone. It was much like the smell that lingers after a heavy rain in summer.

Roz similarly positioned the others, and the three were instructed not to move a muscle.

"What happens now?" Nudge asked through gritted teeth as he stared ahead through the shimmering water.

"Now's the part where you all get rejected," Roz replied derisively.

"Don't call it 'til you see it," Laoch shot back.

HONK HONK HONK went the Wall.

Roz laughed. "Okay kid, whatever you say."

"Just wait until we give the count," the female Guard instructed. "On 'three' you'll step forward one step, and the Shield will enclose you—"

"Will it hurt?!" Leeland fretted.

"You won't feel a thing," she replied tiredly.

"*Then* what do we do?" Nudge asked, his left foot beginning to twitch. He was not used to standing still.

"Stop moving!" Roz barked.

"You do nothing. The Water Shield will do everything. It will know whether or not you are good for the city. If you are meant to be here."

Laoch's heart quickened.

"ONE . . ." she began.

Leeland took a deep breath.

"TWO . . ."

Nudge steeled his gaze.

"THREE."

All three stepped forward gingerly, and before they could process what was happening, or how, they were subsumed into the Shield.

Sty, watching from outside, gasped. It was as if all three of his friends were spun instantly into cocoons, the shapes of their bodies bulging against the force of the water surrounding them.

As soon as this happened, the boys *inside* the Shield became suspended in an array of sensations. The water was nothing like water. It was cool and feather-light, but not wet at all. Their vision went out and their minds grew quiet. Distant sounds and impressions danced before them. Each lost track of time. Strange murmurings reached their ears, posing questions they answered without words.

Yes, Laoch's mind replied to the mind of the Shield, when all at once they were spit out with such force that they tumbled a few feet away on the dusty ground.

"*Ouch!*" Leeland yelped. Nudge curled into a ball, not wanting to know exactly what had happened or where he'd ended up.

Laoch, on the other hand, peered through his fingers (which were covering his face, he was embarrassed to discover), and found himself staring into an outlet within the rocky surface of a wall. It led to a hallway and yet another wall. He hadn't been able to see that on the other side. . . .

His stomach leapt to his throat. He reached instinctively for his amulet, which always helped him steady himself. But as he turned to the side, expecting to see his brother and Nudge, Laoch startled.

He whipped around the other way.

No one.

He spun in a circle, looking for them frantically.

And just as quickly as his hopes had soared, they plummeted.

He was the only one who had made it through.

Back on the Outside, a group of dazed friends and two *very* astonished Guards watched the Water Shield flatten into its normal state.

"*What the—*" Roz gasped, truly shocked.

"I honestly don't know how that happened," the female Guard mumbled. Bewilderment knit her brows into a dark furrow as she gazed through the Shield at the strange young Lizard on the other side.

Laoch remained motionless, not quite believing his eyes. This was not supposed to happen.

"Try to jump through, Nudge! Just give it one try!" he called desperately.

And try Nudge did, but it was to no avail. For though he was a powerful little Meerkat, all muscle under his fluffy fur, and indeed hurled his body at the Shield with all of his might, when he hit his body was instantly—as if by electricity—blown backward, so that he landed with another crash, flat on his back.

He didn't get up at first either.

Laoch watched helplessly until eventually Leeland pulled Nudge to his feet. Sty—who had joined the others as soon as they'd been expelled from the Shield—handed Nudge some water and rubbed the dust off his back.

Laoch watched his friends as they spoke quietly in a huddle, straining to hear what they were saying. He'd never been separated from them before.

And what lay between them? Only a thin sheet of water.

"That's enough of that," Roz said, putting a hand on Nudge's shoulder as if to console him for his pathetic effort. "It's not going to make a difference."

Nudge began to cry.

"I'm sorry, Laoch . . . I don't know why I didn't get in . . . I tried my hardest!"

Upon hearing this, fat tears rolled down Leeland's face as well.

"I'm sorry too," he choked. "I know Father said we had to stay together, but—"

Laoch sank to his knees, his own eyes growing misty. *It was not supposed to happen like this*, he thought over and over.

Even Sty was crying. His feelings had been badly hurt by the Guards, and the whole situation was confusing.

"Alright, enough of this. Better get going, you three," the female Guard urged, her tone a warning.

"But what do we *do*?" Leeland pleaded, worried now to the point of shaking. He had never been without his brother. Who would make decisions about where to go, what to do?

Laoch took a deep breath. He felt responsible for them all, even though he was inside the city and they were not. And now, *especially* now, he had to make things right. For them, for his parents, for everyone.

"I need to do this," he told them, steeling himself. "I have to stay. You know I do. Leeland, remember what Father—"

His brother nodded, emitting a small sob.

"Lee, I need you to know—" Laoch started, but could not finish, for his voice caught in his throat.

The Guards looked down, embarrassed by his florid proclamations.

"Where should we go?" Nudge asked, similarly overtaken. Laoch stood up. *I can't let them down now*, he resolved, wiping his eyes. Then, sounding as confident as he could for their sakes, Laoch came up with a plan.

"The three of you should head west to the Cascade Sea. Find a small town where you can enter safely and stay there. Don't go back to Talamh, whatever you do . . . they may be looking for . . ."

He trailed off, hoping they would understand what he meant. For he could not speak freely in front of the Guards, who, though pretending to give the boys space to talk, were obviously listening with suspicion.

"Send word once you're settled, and I'll come for you. Once I . . . you know . . ."

Again Laoch paused, emphatically patting the pocket that held the golden disc. The other three nodded tearfully. They understood.

Suddenly, Leeland's eyes widened.

"Laoch! Watch out behind you!"

He swung around just as two large military Beings appeared beside him—much older than the other Guards but similarly attired.

"Don't have a spaz attack," Roz muttered. "It's just the other shift. Ours is ending."

The new Guards eyed Laoch distrustfully.

"Who's he?" they inquired. Roz and the female Guard replied in unison that he was a new entry.

"Hhhmmmph," one of them grunted, then scanned his hand on the Wall. The Shield momentarily opened, and the two passed through to the Outside. They exchanged a few formalities before Roz and the female Guard also scanned their hands, traversed the Shield, and joined Laoch on the Inside.

"Let's go buster, we'll lead you in," Roz said tiredly, taking Laoch by the arm. But Laoch jerked away.

He wasn't ready.

"You'll stick to the plan?!" he called desperately to the others.

"Yes!" they replied. "We promise!"

"I'll come for you," Laoch repeated. "If my life depends on it, I'll come for you!"

Behind him, Roz rolled his eyes. But the female Guard stood strangely still, for she was moved by the scene, despite herself.

The three boys on the Outside nodded one last time, and now not knowing what else to do, began to walk away.

"Wait!" Laoch yelled. "I need to give you something, Leeland. It's for good luck!"

Laoch reached deep into one of his pockets and wildly rifled around, finally yanking out a fist. The Guards both Inside and Outside were called to attention. The two brothers ran to each other, poised on either side of the Shield.

The Guards advanced on them, shouting things like:

"Now hold on a second—"

"What do you think you're doing?"

"Get your hand away from the Shield!"

But the boys, acting quickly out of love and a connection that can only really exist between brothers, shot their hands toward the thin barrier between them.

Leeland's hit first. Miraculously, his hand did not bounce back like he expected, but rather penetrated the water easily. Laoch's eyes popped, seeing this, but he acted just as quickly, placing his hand over his brother's. Leeland couldn't be sure he felt something fall into his palm, but retracted it from the water anyway and skittered away from the Shield. For the older Guards were coming at him and they did not seem pleased.

"Did you see that?"

"Did you put your fist through?!"

But Leeland, Nudge, and Sty were already moving swiftly away from the great city. The Guards let them go, leaving well enough alone.

"Man, this thing really *is* on the fritz today," Roz commented, nonplussed by the boys' final act. He and the female Guard took Laoch by the armpits, for suddenly he could not support himself, and began to topple over. His body, limp with exhaustion and excitement, had also started the process of adjusting to the time shift within the city.

"It'll pass in a little while," the female Guard assured him.

Laoch did not hear her, though. His mind was faltering. *"Remember the plan!"* he whispered—to himself, to his brother, and to his friends, who were already making their way back across the Great Plains.

With assistance, Laoch was led down a narrow corridor between two stone walls. His feet fell feebly one after the other, his head hanging on his chest. His vision flickered, his skin tingled. He began to think he might really be in trouble, for he had never felt so terrible in his life. Desperately he wished he had stayed with the others. Surely they could have figured out another plan to help his parents. But then the passageway gently curved and another archway appeared—this one embedded in the Inner Wall. Laoch felt as though he wouldn't even make it that far, for they seemed to be moving impossibly slowly, and his body felt heavier and heavier.

But then, unexpectedly, there it was beside him. The entrance.

He had made it.

He had reached the city. And now he was about to see inside for the very first time.

And so the Guards led him through the door, and a bright scene emerged—one he had spent his entire life imagining.

To

be

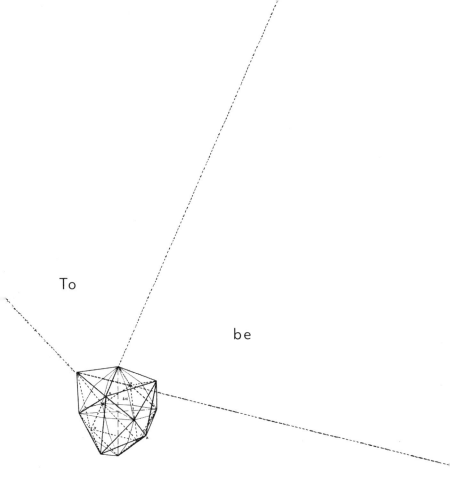

continued . . .

PRONUNCIATION GUIDE

NAME	PRONUNCIATION
ATHAIR	*AHT-her*
CASCADE SEA	*kas-KĀD SĒ*
CIALL	*KĒL*
CREIGHT	*KRĀT*
DOSHA	*DŌ-shuh*
ÈAGRUTHACH	*Ā-gruū-hah*
FAICHILL	*FAH-shil*
FÁSACHLANDS (FÁS)	*FAH-sik-lanz*
FREDERICK (FREDDIE)	*FRED-rik*
GALÁNTA	*guh-LON-tuh*
GREAT PLAINS	*GRĀT PLĀNS*
GUNN	*GUHN*
GUSTAR	*GŪ-ster*
INIS BREAG	*IN-is BRĀG*
IONA	*ī-Ō-nuh*
IRON MOUNTAINS	*Ī-ern MOUWN-tins*
LAOCH	*LĀ-ok*
LEELAND	*LĒ-lind*
MERIDIAN	*mer-RID-ē-an*
MÁTHAIR	*MAHT-her*

Pronunciation Guide

NAME	PRONUNCIATION
MR. MOONGATE	*MIS-ter MŪN-gāt*
NORTHEASTERN WOODLANDS	*nōrth-ĒST-ern WOOD-lindz*
NUDGE	*NUDJ*
OLC	*OLK*
ROZ	*RAHZ*
SCATH MÁTHAIR	*SKAH MAHT-her*
SOUTHERN HILLS	*SUH-thern HILZ*
SPREAG	*SPRAG*
STY	*STĪ*
TALAMH	*TALL-iv*
TIDER	*TĪ-der*
TRAZO BLANO	*TRAH-zō BLAH-nō*
UTOMIA	*ū-TŌ-mē-uh*
WARFORE	*WAHR-for*
WAYLOR	*WĀ-lor*
MS. WHAKDAK	*MZ WAK-dak*
YOSEPH VAN DER MEER	*YŌ-sef VAN der mēr*

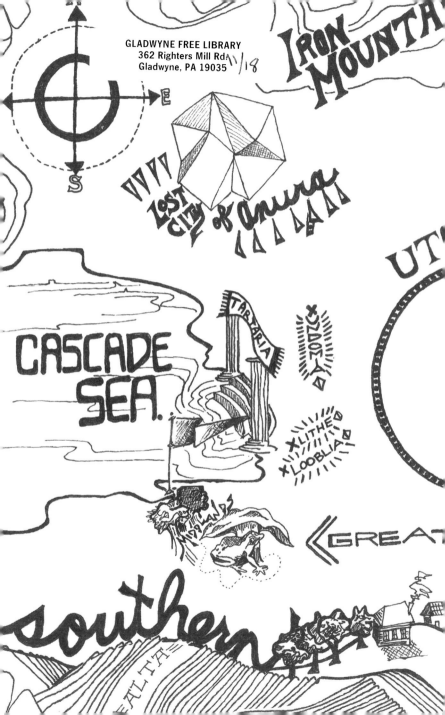